"I CAME TO APOLOGIZE. I'M SORRY YOU HAD TO BE THE ONE TO FIND MY MOTHER THAT WAY."

Martha Hitchcock stood up. The doctor had told her about her mother's suicide—too many pills, too much booze, definitely no accident—but it was Pete who'd explained about finding her in the bath.

Pete shrugged. He put down the ball of twine he'd been fiddling with and began to unroll his shirt cuffs and then roll them back up again.

As she moved toward the door of Pete's office, Martha looked behind her out the window at the marsh. "It's nice here," she said. "I don't know why but the water always looks warmer here than it does out by my house."

Pete looked at Martha. "Hot water," he said.

"What?" She frowned, crumpling her eyebrows.

"Her tub water was hot. Doctor Rogers came, and he said she'd been dead for hours . . . but the water in the tub was still hot! Steaming!"

"She was dead for hours . . ." Martha repeated tonelessly. "But the water was hot."

"She didn't run it herself," said Pete, and he stood up too . . .

HOT WATER

SALLY GUNNING

POCKET BOOKS

New York   London   Toronto   Sydney   Tokyo   Singapore

An *Original* Publication of POCKET BOOKS

 POCKET BOOKS, a division of Simon & Schuster Inc.
1230 Avenue of the Americas, New York, NY 10020

ISBN: 0-671-72804-0

First Pocket Books printing November 1990

10 9 8 7 6 5 4 3 2 1

POCKET and colophon are registered trademarks of
Simon & Schuster Inc.

Printed in the U.S.A.

HOT
WATER

Chapter

1

Peter Bartholomew was having a bad day. He looked at the dead woman floating in the tub, *lolling* in the tub, and tried to remember how much he hadn't liked her the first time he had met her, the day she'd hired him. It didn't help things much. He went into the usual adrenaline-inspired motions; he hauled the slippery, slimy, too-white flesh out of the water and onto the floor, sloshing buckets of water across the yellow tiles and out into the hall.

She appeared to be dead. Very dead. Her face was an odd color, there were dark bruiselike spots along her backside, and she wasn't exactly what you would call limp. But why was she so warm? He left her there on the floor and backed down the stairs to the hall phone to call the emergency number. Jean, the dispatcher, answered—another bad sign.

"This is Peter Bartholomew—"

"Pete! I was just trying to call you at your office. Is that where you are? Your line was busy.

1

I have *got* to have my windows cleaned. And guess who I saw this morning! Connie!''

Peter Bartholomew was suddenly overcome by a fast-moving strain of exhaustion. He sank down onto the bottom stair. Why was everyone so anxious today to tell him his wife was back? "This is an emergency, Jean. I'm at the Hitchcock place—"

"Where?"

"Denault. The Denault place." The dead woman, Edna Denault, had become Edna Hitchcock at least thirty or forty years before, but just try to tell anyone on this island that—especially Jean, especially when you were trying to get her to turn around and holler over her shoulder to the fire department to get the rescue wagon out fast to this house. The fact that Pete and his sister Polly had called this house "The Spookhouse" now seemed a bad, prophetic joke. "She's dead in the tub. Will you get the wagon out here?"

"Hold on," Jean hollered—first into the phone by mistake, then over her shoulder—and then someone who sounded like the police officer Paul Roose hollered back. There was a loud buzz, and a crash, and a tearing sound, and then Jean was back.

"They're on their way. Though what's the rush if she's dead, I couldn't tell you. Drunk? Was she drunk?"

Pete sighed. How was he supposed to know that? It was odds on, of course, and now that he thought about it, hadn't there been a glass there on the floor by the tub? Maybe even a bottle?

"Matter of time," said Jean. "And what are you doing there, anyway?"

Pete explained that Edna Hitchcock had hired

him to catalog some books preparatory to selling them to Jerry Beggs, who ran The Bookworm Shop. That seemed to be enough about Edna.

"Connie's been here since last night and she says she hasn't seen you. You hiding?"

"No," said Pete, but it had been a trying day. Ever since Bert Barker had told him, he'd been doing double takes all over town at every flash of pale hair, at every laugh that began low and sailed high.

"Now, about those windows—"

"We don't do windows," said Pete, which was a lie—there wasn't anything they categorically didn't do. He didn't recall hanging up the phone, or going back up the stairs, or arriving at the body again, or sitting on the floor staring at it, but that's where he was when the police chief, Will McOwat, and the two firemen arrived.

"She's hardening," he said to the chief, and then he got up and hit the stairs two at a time, thinking as he went below that there must be someplace on the island of Nashtoba where his wife, anyone who knew his wife, dead bodies, and Jean's windows would be out of reach. But there was no such place on Nashtoba. He could leave the island, of course, and he considered it—about as long as it took him to round the porch rail and catch a glimpse of the cold, gray waves and the sky with no light in it at all.

Off the corner of the southeast corner of New England a peninsula grows from the main trunk of the continent like a sassafras leaf, forking and dividing halfway out into two smaller peninsulas. One is the smaller version of the other, like the

3

thumb of a mitten, and is closer to sea level—at high tide it connects to the other with nothing but a causeway made of wooden planks. The name for the sassafras leaf as a whole is Cape Hook. There are thirteen towns on Cape Hook, some with Indian names, like Nashtoba and Naushon; some with the names of the early sea captains and settlers, such as Weams Point, or Bradford. Cape Hook is a summer resort. It wasn't always, of course; it was a lot of different things, in layers, depending on who came and moved in on top of whom. The Indians were the bottom layer to the place. They fished there and hunted there and named things there, and then the early settlers came along, and the whalers came along, and the fishermen came along; and they kept the easy Indian names like Arapo and Nashtoba and Naushon and changed the hard ones like Attaconkeet and Motacakanett to things like Murray's Mills and Weams and Bradford. They changed the names of the harbors, too: The harbor on the inland side they called Far Harbor and the harbor on the ocean side Close Harbor. It made sense to them: Close Harbor was away from the mainland but closer to the fishing grounds and old whaling waters. If you shipped out of Close Harbor you just pointed your boat out and went straight; if you shipped out of Far Harbor, you had to go halfway around the Hook before you could head out straight to where you wanted to go. In those days it was all fishing boats in Close Harbor; the few yachts and cabin cruisers hung out in Far Harbor.

After the white men who lived off the sea came the white men who bobbed around its edges—the fry-in-the-sun-capsize-and-scream-"no-underwater"-

4

at-your-kids crowd—the tourists. Once they came, the smarter of the deep-water white men and almost all of the Indians turned their backs on what came from under the sea and started making their living off the creatures that came streaming across the top of it.

The economy flourished, but only for the big part of the mitten. Nashtoba was just one of the thirteen towns on Cape Hook, but because it was the only town in the thumb part of the mitten, the people who lived in the thumb itself came to be known as Nashtobans and began to think of themselves as an island separate from Cape Hook. So did the weather. They had their summer tourists on Nashtoba, but often as not they ended up complaining without ceasing to their hosts—in June they wanted less rain and in July they wanted air conditioners. By August it was already dropping down to forty at night on Nashtoba, and they wanted blankets and portable heaters and a store that sold sweatshirts for less than twenty dollars. Labor Day weekend, the few who remained limped back across the planks to the world of washers and dryers and insulated walls, most never to return, and Nashtoba was left with the oddballs: the old people who no longer worked, the rich people who never had, some fishermen who didn't know of or care for an easier way to do it, arty types who liked the idea of island life but never quite figured out how to live off of it, and the people like Peter Bartholomew, who had.

Twenty years before, Peter Bartholomew was a sixteen-year-old Nashtoba High School sophomore, standing on the marsh and looking back across the causeway toward the Hook, about to cross over and begin the hunt for a summer job in the real world. He was thinking about the expression they had on Nashtoba for what he was about to do: "Walk the plank and become a Hooker." He couldn't do it. He turned around, walked into Beston's Hardware, and bought a marker and a piece of posterboard. One word off his last week's vocabulary quiz popped into his mind, and he wrote across the top of the board in big letters "Factotum"; then under that in smaller print, since he was sure no one but his English teacher knew what the word meant, he wrote "A person employed to do all kinds of work." Then he added his name and phone number and tacked it onto the bulletin board on Beston's porch. Almost every building on Nashtoba had a porch, and everyone hung out on them whenever they could, but Beston's porch was the porch of all porches: Sooner or later, everyone who was not anyone sat down on its pine bench or leaned against its rail and had a cup of coffee or a Coke from the machine that still sold them for a quarter in tall glass bottles. The first few weeks his sign had been up, he mowed a couple of lawns for some summer people who didn't want to, caulked a windowpane for an old woman who couldn't, painted a house for an artist who was meant for other, higher pursuits. Then one of the lawn people, Greg Harrington, asked if he did indeed do "all kinds of work," and Pete answered that he did. Would he pick up Greg's cousin at the airport at 11:53 P.M.? Pete would, and he did. The Harringtons told the Peales, whose son needed tutoring in math, that Factotum did everything. Pete tutored Louis Peale and he passed into the ninth grade. A Mrs. Abrew heard about the Peale boy and called up. Her eyesight was failing and she could no longer read the newspaper, would be happy to pay someone to come in each morning to catch her up on the news. Would he do it? He did. He kept reading to Sarah Abrew before school that fall. He made dump runs and ran errands on weekends. He did yardwork, housework, whatever he had time for; and when he didn't have time for it all he hired his sister Polly to help out.

By the time he'd graduated from college, Pete had hired two additional year-round regulars and a shifting crew of summer help, rented the cottage on the marsh for himself and Factotum, propped his B.A. in history on the shelf, and settled down to business.

Or almost all business. A year later Connie Benz, one of the off-and-on summer crew, graduated from college with a degree in secondary education, propped her degree up next to Pete's, moved into Factotum with him, and became year round. The year after that they got married, bought the cottage, and settled in for keeps. Or at least Pete did.

One day after nine years of what had seemed to Pete a near-perfect marriage, Connie packed up all her personal possessions and at least one of Mrs. Glen Newcomb's personal possessions—Mr. Glen Newcomb—walked the plank, and was gone. Pete had partially filled the hole she had left in his personnel roster with Bill Freed, and was just perfecting the careful sidestep around the hole she had left in his personal life, when Edna Hitchcock died, and Connie came back home, alone.

Chapter
2

Martha Hitchcock drove slowly down the main street of town, the black canvas top of her yellow VW bug folded up like half a bellows, exposing her for all the world to see, the Hooker. Worse than a Hooker. She had left Nashtoba and gone past even the Hook, off into the real world to do it for real money, to work, to play, to hide. She should never have come back. She'd read that somewhere, in some book, someone else had figured that out before her about not coming home; but it was one of those things that you didn't believe yourself until you were driving down Main Street past the library, the town hall, the school, the police and fire, the supermarket, and nothing was changed but you. Or was it? There was the old real-estate office, and the antique store, and the laundromat, but now a *new* real-estate office, and a new bank, and The Bookworm Shop. But again, there was the post-office crowd all bunched up together, and there was Beston's Hardware. All the buildings were either weathered shingles or white clapboards, even the new bank, except for Beston's. Beston's had once been a barn red, but it was now washed out by salt and sun to an orangy pink that stuck out from the rest like a whorehouse in a row of churches, and Martha was drawn to it as any good Hooker would be. Beston's was in the center of Main Street, next to the post office, and that meant it was the center of everything in Nashtoba. The porch of Beston's was always full and the rail wasn't level. Martha had always figured the rail wasn't level because the floor wasn't level; and the floor wasn't level, she figured, because fat Ed Healey always sat on the left. Yes, there he was, fat Ed Healey, and Evan Spender, and Bert Barker, and some others she didn't recognize. She drove by in weather too cold for the top to be down and watched them watch her, all eyes straight ahead and whispered comments passing from sides of mouths like sparks. "That's the Hitchcock girl," maybe, or " 'Bout time she showed up." Someone was bound to be saying "What's she showing up now for, just 'cause her mother's dead? Didn't show for her own father's funeral now, did she?" Later, after she had driven on past, they'd remember other things and really get down to it: the congressman, the school trouble, Joe Weams . . . She turned left off Main Street, scooted around a frost heave and listened to her tires make that silky sound as they hit a patch of sand. Scrub pines, residential houses, then the once-white, now mildew-gray sign: "Hardiman Rogers, M.D." She parked the VW beside his maroon Volvo station wagon and got out.

There was a pregnant woman in the waiting

room, changing positions in her chair like a hen on a nest. And a new secretary. Martha gave her name to the unknown face before her and asked if she could make an appointment.

A young mother and little boy came down the hall, and there he was behind them—a looming, six-foot Mark Twain with wild white hair, steel-gray thundercloud eyebrows, and lightning-blue eyes. He saw her.

"You here to see me?"

"No rush," said Martha.

"Wait," he barked at her, and then he herded the pregnant woman in front of him down the hall.

She waited. The pregnant woman soon returned and stood at the desk to make her next appointment. Hardy Rogers snapped out a few more things for his secretary to do: order lytes on Winchester, give Percy two refills on Xanax, try one more time to get hold of Burkett. Then he turned and waved Martha into the hall in front of him—not into the examination room but past it into his office, the oppressively dark wood walls and creaking chairs making her more nervous than the examination room ever did. They sat facing each other across his desk. Hardy Rogers laid his forearms across the leather desktop, and Martha looked at the starched sleeves of his lab coat. Still an old-fashioned starch lover. His hands were large and hairy, and they lay comfortably on the desk. Martha, not knowing what to do with hers, began to crumple them into a ball in her lap.

"Wasn't sure you'd come back," said Hardy.

Martha shrugged, looking down.

"I've been hearing things about you. 'Bout time you came home."

I'm not home, she wanted to say. I'm just here. And I have to go. Soon. She said nothing.

"Well, you look like hell, if you don't mind my saying so. You sick? That why you're here?"

Martha shook her head.

"You want to know about your mother," said Hardy, and Martha looked up. The blue eyes seemed to fine-tune their focus on her face, scanning it back and forth.

"She died," said Hardy, "from too much alcohol and too many pills. Seconal. And just for the record, I wouldn't fill that Seconal prescription the last time she asked, and she fired me over it. The cops couldn't find the bottle, but I checked around. Brixton gave it to her."

Martha wondered what Hardy must have thought about her mother's death. That her mother took the pills and drank the booze on purpose? And what did "on purpose" mean, exactly? Someone says "Today I think I'll die." Or someone says, not out loud or even to oneself, "What do I care?" Or "Who will be hurt?"

Martha said, "I heard once that if you take Seconal for a long time you run the risk of it accumulating. One day you take one that turns out to be the one too many."

Hardy shook his head. "No. This was no accident, and if it's any consolation, it wasn't one of those lingering coma deals, either. It was one big dose and about ten fingers of bourbon. She went out fast, Martha, and she took nobody with her. You can thank her for that; it could have been worse."

Thank her; it could have been worse.

"You'll be staying at the house?"

Martha looked away. "No. I called Hillerman's and they hadn't rented the boathouse yet, so I paid them for the summer."

But I won't be staying the summer out. Or will I?

After a silence of indeterminate length, during which Hardy did nothing but look at her, Martha spoke again. "Who found her?"

"Peter Bartholomew," said Hardy. "Factotum. He was due out on a job; she'd given him the key. Said she wasn't going to be on the island for a few days. He did what he could, but she'd been dead several hours by then. . . ."

Peter Bartholomew. Factotum. If that wasn't Nashtoba for you, nothing was. It did cross her mind as she pushed back her chair and thanked Dr. Rogers that he would find it odd that she was laughing.

Chapter
3

Pete was seeing her again. He knew he was not asleep, but still he could not derail her image from his brain. Her two images. The one, the first time they had met: a pressed and polished woman in her late fifties, the silver-gold hair skinned back from her face and coiled at the nape of her neck, looking like the motor that made the head turn. Left, right, center; around the attic, looking at the books.

"Some of these may be worth something," she had said, but not as if she really cared. Her dress, that first day, had been a white wool, her skin almost clear, her eyes only barely green and without expression. Odd that she would look so much like a ghost that first time he had seen her, when she had been alive. He had thought at first she was wearing very old perfume and had then wised up: It was very fresh bourbon.

The second time he had seen her ... He wrenched his eyes open and threw off the sheet and blanket and stood in the middle of the room

13

and looked at it. There was his stereo at one end, the fold-out couch he slept in at the other, and off the back was the porch and off the porch was the marsh and off the marsh was the Sound. . . . He walked over to the highboy and fished out clean jockey shorts and socks and headed for the shower. The second time he had seen her . . . something was funny about it. *Something*.

It was eight-thirty when he pushed open the door between his kitchen and what used to be the rest of his house but was now Factotum. Eight-thirty, and Rita Peck was there already. Rita, who had been hired ten years before for what at the time seemed the simple job of answering the phone, was now a partner in Factotum and the one, practically speaking, who ran it. She also, since her divorce—and more especially since his—occasionally tried to run Pete.

"When I *ask* you to call me, I mean I *want you to call me,*" Rita was spitting into the phone. "If I didn't mean it when I said it, I'd *tell* you I didn't mean it!"

Rita was talking to her fifteen-year-old daughter, Maxine, and Pete had been observing that Maxine had discovered two things of late: that the best defense was a good offense, and that any product of a broken home who didn't learn how to work one parent off against the other was nuts. Pete peeked around the hall corner and looked at Rita. Her short black hair was bobbing and gleaming like a crow's wing, her eyebrows were buckled into a knot, and her brown eyes were looking black: all signs that things were getting close to serious. It was not a morning, Pete decided, to slip out back to the marsh as he had been contemplating doing.

He approached Rita's desk, which was crammed into the corner of what was once his living room, and sat down on its edge. He gave Rita the thumbs-up sign. Her eyebrows nearly crossed each other.

"You're going to stay in until I say you can go out. Until I say so. I don't care if he *is* fairer, he has a lot less hours he has to be fair *in*. No. No! If I come home and find one hair on your head not its natural color . . ." Rita rolled her eyes at Pete and, in the course of the roll, caught something in them and focused on it in such a way that it caused Pete to turn.

A woman was standing in the doorway. He knew who she was, not only because he literally did know who she was, but because now she was a familiar ghost: a more youthful, living version of the face he had seen dead in the tub—Martha Hitchcock, Edna's daughter. But this reincarnation of the dead woman was unlike her in some ways: Her denim skirt had been hemmed with a pair of scissors, her sleeves were rolled up, her hair was sliding out of its pins, and her leather sneakers were scuffed. He remembered Edna's well-kept beauty the day they'd spoken in the attic, and where Edna Hitchcock had been meticulously made up, her daughter wore nothing on her face but straight bones, green eyes, and pale skin that was growing paler. She didn't give a damn if anyone thought her attractive, and Pete discovered at that minute that it was that very fact that made him find her so. Very much so. He stepped forward and introduced himself, unsure if she would remember him from brief island encounters, and then he looked around. She would want to talk to him about her mother, he guessed, but not here in the middle of *Teen Tramp Meets the Mother Monster*. He motioned behind him and began to back up into what had once been an office of sorts but was now full of the odds and ends that made up Factotum. He stepped around a garden hose, over a bag of peat, under a beach umbrella, and, scooping a pile of newspapers off the one chair, offered it to Martha. Pete overturned a small wheelbarrow and sat down on that.

"You found her," said Martha.

Pete nodded.

"You just showed up at her house at seven o'clock at night?"

Pete looked at the green eyes and down again, embarrassed. How to explain the cloying depression that had struck him and driven him out of this house that he had once found so friendly and warm? How to make his seven-o'clock trip to her mother's attic sound more . . . normal? "I've been pretty busy during the day," he began. "It seemed like good work for nighttime, cataloging the books up there in the attic; Jerry Beggs had made her an offer—"

"She was selling my father's books," said Martha, and Pete, looking at her, saw an expression he had come to know quite well from morning glances in his own mirror: hurt, big-time hurt, the kind that comes with surprises. He wanted to say he was sorry, but instead he picked up a ball of twine and began to wind it up.

"She said she was moving. I was on my way up to the attic when I saw the bathroom door open, and there she was in the tub. She'd said she was going to be away. I would have knocked if I—"

"In the tub?" Martha was frowning. "She was in the tub?"

Pete began to explain. All of a sudden there was a splintering sound from behind Martha that sent both of them up onto their feet. Bill Freed stood in the doorway, a fragment of the doorjamb affixed to the corner of a large metal toolbox he held in his hand. When Pete had first met Bill Freed he'd added up his six-foot–four-inch frame with a chin and shoulders straight out of a Marlboro ad and dubbed him Superman; three broken lawn mowers and two new fenders later, he'd concluded he was a cleverly disguised Clark Kent instead. The damaged doorway didn't surprise him; the fact that Bill Freed was fast turning the color of cooked salmon did.

"Hey, don't worry about it," said Pete, and he introduced Martha.

"Pleased to meet you," she said.

Bill didn't speak.

Now what the hell is the matter with him? wondered Pete. "Did you need me, Bill?"

"No," said Bill, but he didn't move.

"Okay then . . ."

Still nothing.

Martha turned her back on him and resumed her seat in the chair. There was a minor rasping sound of steel on brass doorknob, and then Bill Freed was gone, and at once Martha stood up again.

"Thank you," she said to Pete. "I just wanted to say . . . thank you. And I'm sorry. I'm sorry you had to be the one to find my mother that way. Hardy Rogers told me that you tried to do what you could, and I . . ."

Pete coughed and pushed his hands through his

hair. He put down the twine and began to unroll his shirtcuffs but then decided against it and rolled them back up.

As she moved toward the door, Martha looked behind her out the window at the marsh. "It's nice here," she said. "The water here looks . . . warmer. Warmer than it does at . . . at my house."

Pete looked at her. "Warmer," he said.

"I know it isn't, I—"

"Hot water," he said.

"What?"

"Her tub water was hot. Hardy Rogers came, and he said she'd been dead for hours. But the water in the tub was still hot. Steaming."

"She was dead for hours . . ." Martha repeated. She wasn't getting it.

"She didn't run that hot water herself," said Pete, and he stood up too.

Chapter
4

Pete looked across the huge desk that only partly camouflaged the hulking chief and wondered if it was just that the chief was too new, too off-island, to be ready to listen to someone like him, or if he just wasn't saying it right.

"The water was *hot,*" he said again, and he wondered if he should explain to the chief that he was too new, but he guessed he already knew it—suspected that Paul Roose, who had been passed over in favor of this cop from Boston, had already made it clear in a hundred or so different ways. Sometimes Pete hated Nashtoba.

"She'd been dead for hours; Hardy said so. My bathwater doesn't stay hot that long, Chief, does yours?"

Will McOwat ran his hand through his hair, or what there was of it, and Pete took a minute to be grateful that he wasn't one of those balding men who parted his hair over one ear and combed the long stray ends all the way over the top.

"What are you saying here?" asked the chief,

looking sideways at Martha in a way that made Pete feel oddly unsettled.

"Foul play," said Martha, and she gave a ghoulish laugh that frightened all three of them.

Pete cleared his throat. "I know that it all seemed . . . accidental at the time, and the reason it seemed so was because I wasn't paying attention to the water. But dead women don't rise up several hours later and run hot water for a bath, do they? Live men and women don't run hot water over a dead corpse because they want to warm it up, do they?" All of a sudden Pete remembered that this was Martha's mother he was talking about, and he looked at her with concern, but she seemed to be watching him with detachment, an expression of mild interest on her face—but somehow it didn't seem to be interest in *what* he was saying, so much as it was interest in . . . interest in what? Pete didn't know. He gave up and looked back at the chief, and he was surprised to see almost the same expression on his face as well.

"We'll have to get back in the house," the chief said to Martha, and Pete sighed with relief. His job was done.

"Of course, I will have to ask you to keep out of the house for the time being, Ms. Hitchcock, but I will let you know just as soon as we're through over there." The chief rose from behind the desk, and Pete was surprised, seeing him this close for the first time—or at least the first time when he was in a position to notice these things—how big he was. He looked like a rain barrel propped on telephone poles, and beside him, Martha instinctively backed up.

*   *   *

Martha thought the chief could have no idea how gratefully she received his request to stay out of her mother's house. She had arrived here on Nashtoba expecting to face the task of clearing out her mother's house, putting her mother's affairs in order, and no one but herself could ever guess how much she dreaded the job. She hated that house so much. She hated Nashtoba. Then again, sometimes she loved it too much, and Martha didn't like to love things; it was something that had never paid off well in the past, and whenever she felt the risk of love for this place getting strong she would purposely go away and stay away for a spell. Now she couldn't leave here, but at least she was able to postpone returning to that house for a while, thanks to Peter Bartholomew. Or should she be thanking him? Thanks to him, something everyone had bought as a self-inflicted death was about to be considered murder. Still, she felt an odd sense of relief over it all, which was very strange—a relief that this news was out, once and for all. Martha rose from her chair along with the chief and Peter Bartholomew, watched the chief shake first Pete's hand and then hers, and walked between them toward the door. She looked sideways at Peter Bartholomew. Walking next to the chief he looked small, but measuring him up next to her own small frame, she realized that he must be almost six feet tall, if you added an inch for the way he'd rumpled up his reddish-brown hair so that it stood up in spikes. Peter Bartholomew kept looking sideways at her, checking in to make sure she was all right, his soft brown eyes saying way too much and saying it much too often. He periodically gave her a small smile, an eye-smile; he didn't seem to realize he had a perfect set of teeth. Martha wondered if he remembered the last time he had seen her, and she started to smile, remembering it herself, and only stopped when she became aware that Peter Bartholomew was the second person in two days who had caught her doing that and was looking at her strangely.

She had returned to Nashtoba because she had been missing the house, but almost from the minute she entered, she began to hunt for an excuse to get out. The fight with her mother had dragged out into extra innings, and by the time Martha remembered that there was a twentieth anniversary party for Factotum she could hide out in, the party was already well underway.

She knew no one and everyone—knew who they were but didn't want to speak to them or doubted they wanted to speak to her—and she began to wander aimlessly, wondering when her mother would pass out and it would be safe to go home. She saw an old woman sitting on the rattan couch and, recognizing her as Mrs. Abrew, moved over toward her to say hello. Mrs. Abrew was clutching a glass of clear fluid in which floated a single cube of ice; Martha doubted the glass was filled with water. Mrs. Abrew, despite her questionable eyesight, recognized Martha at once and called her by name.

"I'm sorry about your mother," she said to Martha, and Martha got nervous. It was her father who had died. The old lady was losing it. Martha said "Thank you" and moved off into the crowd.

She saw Peter Bartholomew attempting to cross the room toward Mrs. Abrew, Rita Peck buzzing around him like a fly. Several women attempted to waylay his progress, but he didn't seem to notice. Then Martha turned and saw Bill Freed, and, remembering it, she had to laugh, again. He had dropped his glass, stepped on Rita Peck's foot, and backed into a good-looking woman with red hair who turned out to be his wife, Adrienne. An eighth of a teaspoon of wine trickled over the edge of her glass and onto her blouse, and she shrieked "Clod!" with just enough decibels to attract the attention of the nearest quarter of the party. "God, why do I put up with you!"

Martha remembered wondering the reverse.

"Now I have to go change," Adrienne Freed continued. "No!" she snapped, to something mumbled by Bill. "I don't want you near me! Back? To this? I don't think so!"

Bill Freed mumbled something else and looked around, probably for Peter Bartholomew, afraid he had heard, and Adrienne hissed on: "That's up to you! Walk, for all I care!" and she left him.

Martha bent down beside Bill Freed to help him pick up the broken glass and saw that his face was near purple in what she had assumed at the time was fury but learned later was more likely to have been shame.

"Don't get mad, get even," said Martha. Slowly the head near hers raised up to meet her eyes. His eyes were an unusual midnight shade of blue that went well with his dark hair.

"I'm leaving soon myself," said Martha, "and would be happy to give you a ride."

They spent the night on the Hook, in Arapo, in a twenty-dollar room at the Port-O-Call.

*   *   *

They never met on Nashtoba, seldom even on the Hook. He concocted excuses for the long ride to Boston and back in one night, and eventually he got more bold, inventing a course in the city that would have him in classes all day Saturday and in the library all Sunday. He began arriving Friday night and leaving early Monday morning, barely in time to arrive at Factotum by nine. As Bill Freed's Kentish cocoon began cracking, strange things began happening to Martha. She felt anger when she found him leaving a second razor in her medicine cabinet. She felt annoyance when he contradicted her over the best way to cook rice. When he overheard her fighting with her mother on the phone and expressed shock and disapproval over the things she had said, she had left the apartment shaking with rage. Then Peter Bartholomew found her mother dead in the tub, and Nashtoba and Bill Freed and all her life behind her and before her began to close in.

Martha was sitting on the cot covered with an Indian-print spread that served as her couch. She was staring at the floor, not staring at the floor, her eyes unfocused and her mind too focused, when she heard steps on the outside stairs. Bill, she thought. He'd found out where she was staying, and in half an hour it would be all over the island that she was having an affair with Adrienne Freed's husband, and Adrienne would . . . What would Adrienne do? Martha stood up and ran both her hands through her hair. Bill's wife was Bill's problem. If he was going to be so dumb . . .

There were two sets of feet on the stairs. Bill *and* Adrienne. Bill being dragged up the stairs by

24

the hair of his head . . . Oddly, this thought didn't frighten Martha half as much as the thought of Bill alone. The glass panes in the kitchen door rattled with a knock. Martha hugged her flannel shirt around her and walked through the kitchen up to the door. She saw the police chief and Paul Roose crunched together on the landing outside.

"Sorry to bother you, Ms. Hitchcock," said the chief. "We wondered if we could speak with you a minute. You know Paul?"

Martha and Paul nodded stiffly to each other, Martha wondering if this were going to be an arrest. She had read somewhere that most crimes were solved within twenty-four hours, and if this were true, then these guys were overdue.

"Come in," she said. She looked at Paul Roose as they passed. He looked older, close to sixty now, hair total snow and deep ridges cutting his face into geometric patterns. He would never be chief, Martha realized—not if Will McOwat lasted another few years at least, and the chief couldn't be much past forty. Martha sat on the cot again, and the chief sat in the chair that everyone on Nashtoba called a porch chair, while the rest of the world called it a Kennedy rocker. The chief leaned forward so that his gut expanded and propped itself on his thighs, locking him in so he didn't rock. Paul Roose remained standing, and he looked around.

"As I told you we would, Ms. Hitchcock, we went back into your mother's house, and we found a few things. I was hoping you could help us out with some of them."

Martha began to say something, something not at all what she was expected to say, but halfway through her partially formed thoughts she ran out of steam and gave up, and she leaned back and listened.

"I wondered if you could tell us please when you last visited your mother at her house?"

It would have been embarrassing, if getting embarrassed were still something Martha did. When *had* she last visited her mother? When had that party at Factotum been? "A long time ago," she answered.

"Days? Weeks? Months?"

Nice of him not to add *years,* thought Martha. "Many months," she answered. It would cover a lot of ground.

The chief looked down at a manila folder in his hand and flipped it open. "Did you and your mother get along all right, Ms. Hitchcock?"

Paul Roose began staring intently at the rafters. Goddamn this island, thought Martha; she should have known someone would tell him. A flood of antagonism way out of proportion to the crime filled Martha.

She looked straight at the chief and answered, "No."

Paul Roose fished out a small notebook and wrote something in it. "Hates mother"? wondered Martha, or "Buy beer"? His face was expressionless, but somehow she could tell he was miserable: how he must hate playing lackey to the fat man! Her attention was called back to the matter at hand by the chief.

"We found this in your mother's living room. On the desk. Have you ever seen this before?"

Martha took the paper from the chief's fingers and noted how small her own hand looked, how

26

white next to the weathered brown. He was a big man, but still she could tell by the way he handed her the letter that he was not used to counting on his size to bring people down. She looked at the paper. It was a letter, on tissue-thin blue paper. She read it.

Dear Lizzie,

I've had a day to think since we talked and I feel more than ever that this baby is a good thing. I know it's harder for you, being there with everyone you know, but you couldn't sit where I am day after day seeing all these lives lost without wanting to add one back. There must be a way to get me home and get us married. I'll call you. I'm sorry about what I said on the phone about doing something else—even if it weren't too late I wouldn't want to, not any more, not after thinking about it and hearing your voice. As a matter of fact, I'm getting pretty damned excited, and not just because I'll be getting out of Korea! I'll call you. I love you. I know I never said that before but I think I do. I mean that. I love you!

Hal

After what he felt must have been sufficient time, during which Martha had read the letter through twice, the chief spoke again.

"Have you seen this letter before?"

Martha shook her head.

"Do you know who these people are?"

She shook her head again. Behind the chief, Paul Roose coughed. Was that a warning?

"My mother had a sister named Elizabeth," said Martha. "I think she died before I was born. She drowned. I think they did call her Lizzie." "Poor Lizzie," to be exact.

"Do you know who this Hal might be?"

Martha shook her head.

"Do you remember anything else about your aunt? Was she married? Did she have children?"

Martha shook her head. "That's what's funny. Maybe this is a different Lizzie. She couldn't have married or had children; there is no one in my family besides my . . ." Martha turned sideways and looked out her tiny window at the harbor. How strange, she thought. There is no one now but me.

"You don't recall your parents speaking of this Lizzie? If you could take a minute and think back . . ."

She had already done so, and she remembered once when she had stayed out too late with Joe Weams and her mother and father had gone into their room to discuss what punishment would best suit her crime. It had taken only a short time for her mother's voice to rise loud enough to fill the hall, and for the voice of her father to become emphatic enough so that Martha could hear him as well. Finally her father, his voice half humoring, half needling, had tried to calm her mother down. "You're acting as crazy as Lizzie," he had said; then Martha's mother had hit him. Martha had heard it, the slap, had heard the silence, had heard her father's voice sounding as it had never sounded before. "That's the last time you'll do that, Edna." He had left the house and stayed gone for three days, and Martha could still remember the fear of it, the fear that he would never come back, that she would be left there all alone with *her*. . . .

"She was crazy," said Martha. "I remember them saying she was crazy; nothing else."

The chief shifted in his chair, returned the letter to the manila folder, and cleared his throat. "Your mother died, as far as the medical examiner can determine, on June 15, between the hours of ten A.M. and two P.M. Could you tell me please, just as a matter of routine, where you were on June 15?"

"In Boston," said Martha. "I live there."

"Are you employed, or—"

"I am not presently employed," Martha answered stiffly and thought: I am living off my father's fortunes. "I was at home."

"Alone?"

Martha could see Bill Freed, coming out of the bathroom in too-short pajama bottoms, looking at his watch and saying "I'm going to be late again." He could vouch for her until . . . no. Bill Freed's wife may be *his* problem, but this was hers. "Alone," said Martha. "All day."

"Thank you, Ms. Hitchcock," said the chief. "If you remember later that someone might have seen you—a mailman, perhaps—something like that, I would appreciate a call. Now, could I be so trite as to ask after your mother's enemies?"

Enemies. The word seemed to have no place on this island; it belonged back in Boston, or out among global conflicts. It wasn't a matter of enemies with her mother, it was a matter of what her mother could have said, surely must have said, to

29

any number of people on any number of days that would have pushed them over the edge. It wasn't a question of enemies per se. . . . Martha shook her head and stood up, but since the chief didn't follow, she sat back down, resentfully.

"Your mother's drinking habits," he continued.

Martha's eyes narrowed. "I am not familiar with my mother's habits."

Paul Roose was writing.

"Medications?"

"I am not—"

"You were aware that your mother took sleeping pills?"

"I was not."

Now the chief stood up. "Thank you, Ms. Hitchcock. Now, if we might just look at your car on the way out . . ."

"My car?"

"We found several sets of tire tracks in your mother's drive. These gravel drives are good for that; there is always a place where the gravel has worn out and we're left with dirt. In June on Nashtoba I suppose the proper word is *mud*." He smiled at her.

Martha did not smile back. She felt oddly insulted.

"Of course, we would expect to find certain tracks: Peter Bartholomew's, your mother's own. And when did you say you were last at the house?"

Martha was losing track fast. What had she said? "I wasn't there recently enough for you to have to worry about mine," she answered.

They were all standing now.

"Just the same, we'll take a brief look, if you

30

don't mind. And thank you, Ms. Hitchcock. You have been most helpful. I know this is not an easy time. If you find that we can be of help to you, will you call us?''

Martha didn't answer him right away. She was unable to shift back and forth from offense to defense to neutrality the way he could. "I'd like to keep the letter."

The chief looked at Paul Roose.

"We have a copy," said Paul. "And the lab is finished with it."

The chief opened the folder and handed the letter to Martha. "Don't say I never gave you anything." He grinned.

Fat people always think they're so goddamned jolly, Martha thought.

Chapter 5

Peter Bartholomew sat at his kitchen table looking down at his legal pad, underlining some things, crossing out others, making notes in the margins. "Alcohol, barbiturates," he wrote, and later on, "hot water." How long *did* water stay hot? Pete jumped up from the table and went through to the bath and began filling the tub with hot water. What was it Hardy had said? When Pete pulled Edna out of the tub she had been dead for hours. How many hours? Why would someone fill the tub with hot water? How long did it take a person to die from what everyone on Nashtoba now knew was too much booze with too many pills?

Pete shook his head. This was now none of his business. So what if he found the woman? So what if Martha . . . So what if he was the one who'd caught on to the hot water? Hardy hadn't noticed it; that was for sure. Or had he? What if Hardy had known all along but just didn't want to stir up any trouble? Pete felt a sudden need to talk to

Hardy. He picked up the phone to make an appointment with Hardy for the end of the afternoon.

It wasn't easy to relax in a doctor's waiting room: Around him were a fat lady who was sweating and a little girl who was whimpering. Pete vaguely recognized the fat lady, but he didn't look at her twice so he wouldn't have to talk. He picked up a health magazine from the rack, and by the time Hardy got around to him Pete was convinced that what Hardy had once told him was tendinitis of the elbow was really Lyme disease and would soon have affected every single one of his joints. He limped after Hardy down the hall, and they sat across Hardy's desk and looked at each other.

"I'm not here about my health," said Pete quickly, before Hardy could move him into the other room and have him down to his shorts.

The sharp blue eyes shifted focus slightly. "You made me out for a fool; you know that, I guess. Horned your way in over the station and caused everyone a whole hell of a lot of trouble."

"Did you know about the water? You knew it was hot?"

Hardy slammed his hands down on the leather blotter on his desk, seemingly pleased with the cool-sounding *thwap!* "Of course not! Use your noodle! If I knew it was hot I'd of said it was hot, and I'd of said a few other things besides. There was no water in her lungs; she didn't drown. She stopped breathing. Any old horse's ass could have looked at her and looked at her history and assumed what I assumed: She took some pills and drank herself to—"

There was a timid knock at the closed office

33

door, and Pete, looking across the desk at the glare that would have nailed anything in front of it to the back side of the door, felt sorry for whoever it was on the other side.

The door opened a crack. "I'm sorry, Dr. Rogers," said the secretary, "but I—"

"This won't take a minute," said a voice with considerable resonance, and a good two-thirds of the bulk of the police chief came oozing through the door, followed, once the secretary had retreated, by the remaining third. He seemed surprised to see Pete.

"I'll shove off," said Pete. "I just wanted to check in about the—"

"Sit where you are! You and I aren't finished yet. I'm sure this gentleman has nothing to say to me that can't be said in front of you. Hell, you might add something. Right, Chief?"

The chief looked at the doctor and then at Pete, and it seemed to Pete that he was starting to learn about this place. The smooth oval of his face creased up a little. "Right," he said.

"Pete here wants to know if I knew the water was hot. That what you want to know? I didn't. Anything else?"

The chief picked up a pile of medical journals and a trail of EKG paper off the one remaining chair, pulled it up closer to the desk, and sat down. "Among other things. You did not know the water was hot—did not realize it, shall we say? You do not, however, doubt that what Pete here says is true: that the—"

The hand struck leather again. "If he says it was hot it was hot, goddammit! I don't have time to waste doing things twice. Is that all, sir?"

He was somehow able to deemphasize the *sir* just enough for them to be left with a hint of a question.

"No," said the chief. "About Seconal."

He asked about lethal doses, and Hardy rambled on about Seconal and Pete didn't pay complete attention, more fascinated by the colors and shapes of the words being tossed back and forth around him, until Martha's name was tossed into the pot to boil.

"So you did not prescribe this last batch of Seconal for Edna Hitchcock. Did you ever prescribe any for her daughter, Martha?"

Pete sat up at once.

Hardy leaned forward in his chair. He spoke softly, and the ramifications of what he was saying never seemed to dawn on him until it was too late, and all of Pete's openings and closings of his mouth couldn't stop him.

"I did not," said Hardy. "And if you're taking this in the direction you seem to be taking it, I will tell you to turn around and turn around fast. Martha Hitchcock had nothing to do with Seconal. She didn't like Seconal, and it was she who came to me last May with a bottle she had removed from her mother's house, asking me about its effects and requesting that I give her mother no more. She told me that since her father died her mother was drinking too much. That was all I needed to hear. I discontinued the prescription." He leaned back in his chair, seeming pleased to have so neatly removed Martha from the chief's Seconal list. Obviously, Pete could see him thinking that no one would attempt to keep her mother from overdosing and then go on to overdose her herself.

"That bottle that Martha Hitchcock brought you," said the chief. "She left it here?"

Too late. It was too late by then. Hardy could have lied, Pete supposed, but he knew by now that Hardy was not a lying man. His patients could have told the chief that also: Too often they were told the truth, and too often they were not told it softly.

Martha had left the doctor's office with the bottle. And now the chief knew it. And now he was going to wonder where it went, and he was going to have to wonder if it wasn't sloshing around in a jar someplace, labeled "contents of Edna Hitchcock's stomach."

When Pete got back to Factotum, he noticed by the clock that he had been gone just under two hours. He walked into the bathroom and touched the tub water: It was cold.

It wasn't fifteen minutes later that the police chief's red-and-white Scout with the red bulb on top pulled up in front of Factotum.

"You were next on the list," he said to Pete once they were both inside. "Just a few more questions in light of recent . . . developments, Mr. Bartholomew."

Pete winced. " 'Pete,' please. I hate those things they stick in front of names."

And so did Connie, he thought. Especially the "Mrs." in front of "Peter Bartholomew."

" 'Pete' it will be," said the chief, all in good cheer. In such good cheer, in fact, that Pete doubted he knew what they all called *him*: "The Big Bean"—in honor of his size and his Boston roots. It wasn't exactly an honor, of course; not on Nashtoba.

Pete led his guest back into the room in which he had spoken to Martha and watched him look around with interest. Pete's mind was racing—racing, he was slightly alarmed to realize, in a desperate search for ideas that would divert the chief from bothering Martha. Why? Why was he so concerned about this person he hardly knew? What was it about her that had him charging to her defense for no reason other than . . . other than what? Other than nothing. He cleared his mind, or tried to, and listened to the chief.

"We have to go over a few things again. Sorry. I know this is a pain, but now I need to ask you what you can remember about what you did in the house the day you found Edna Hitchcock, particularly in the bathroom. What, exactly, in the bathroom did you touch?"

Pete frowned. The bathroom, and the blotchy, pale woman, came surfacing once again.

"Specifically, did you wipe anything off?"

"No."

"Nothing? You didn't wipe up any water, use the toilet . . ."

Use the toilet! "No," said Pete, "I didn't." He went over again what he could remember of what he had touched (Edna), what he had moved (Edna!), where he had gone (down, out, away). Eventually.

"You didn't wipe up any water?"

"No." He was sure he hadn't. He remembered it spilling and sloshing all over, and he remembered the rest of them paddling through it.

"The reason I ask," said the chief, "is because

almost every surface in the bathroom had been wiped. Leaving your prints and my prints and the prints of the firemen on top of a perfectly clean slate. We matched them all up, except for one print from the underside of the toilet seat."

"I didn't use the toilet," said Pete. He was about to burst out laughing. As if he would have taken time out to pee!

"You didn't touch the liquor bottle or the glass? You didn't happen to wash them up or . . ."

Wash them up! "No. I didn't touch them at all, unless I knocked into them when I hauled her out. I didn't pick them up, that's for sure."

The chief wrote something in a small notebook. He then removed something from the back of it and handed it to Pete. It was a photocopy of a letter, and it began with "Dear Lizzie" and was signed "Hal."

"Did you see this when you were there?"

Pete read the letter, frowning. He had no idea what was going on here, but all he could do was take it a question at a time. "Did I see this at the house?"

"Yes. Either time. Either the time when she hired you or the time when you found her on the fifteenth."

Pete thought back to the first time, to that awful trip to the attic, and then to the second time, and the worse trip to the bath. He hadn't seen any letter. "No," he answered.

"You didn't see a blue piece of paper on a desk in the living room? Think, please, Pete. This is important."

Pete frowned, thinking. Had he gone into the living room at all, either time? He was sure he hadn't. He didn't even know what the living room looked like. He had gone straight up the stairs.

Pete was getting a headache. He leaned his head on his hand, hoping the chief would assume it was the great weight of his brain that required this extra support, but the chief didn't seem to get the significance. He was looking, if anything, annoyed.

"Think!" he barked, and Pete dropped his hand and looked up, surprised.

"Sorry." The chief took back the letter and put it away. "No excuse. Three lousy cops in the whole department."

"Doesn't the state come charging down in cases like this?" asked Pete, hoping that this guy knew enough to have called them.

The chief shrugged. "We used their lab and tech crews, then I told them to butt out. I can handle this myself." He flipped some pages in his notebook, and Pete watched him. Yes, he thought, he would be thinking of this as his big test. Pete didn't have the heart to tell him that he could solve a hundred murders all by himself and he would still—always, here—remain The Big Bean. From Someplace Else. Pete wondered what weakness or perverseness or having-it-in-for-Paul-Roose had prompted the selectmen to hire The Bean in the first place.

"I didn't see the letter at the house," said Pete.

The chief sighed. "Okay. Now we come to where you were on the fifteenth of June previous to the hour of seven P.M. when you found the body."

Pete's mouth fell open. He was beginning to regret telling this man he could call him by his first name. Pete took the pad out of his hand and went out to Rita's desk and flipped pages in the daily calendar and began writing things down, thinking, writing, until he was left with about ten minutes around noon, at which time, he recalled, he had been sharing fried chicken with Rita at her desk. Rita watched him, puzzled. When he finished, he handed the page to her and had her check it over; and Rita, looking somewhat like an enraged hen whose eggs were just ripped out from under her, signed across the bottom in a flourish that this statement was true and attested to by Rita M. Peck. Pete signed below it.

The chief, watching from the corner of the desk, accepted the paper, said "thank you" very gravely, and waved Pete back into the tiny office.

For God's sake, thought Pete, you mean we aren't done yet? But when the chief spoke again, it was, oddly, to ask him—Pete—his opinion.

"So what do you make of it?"

Pete coughed. "About the . . ."

"Let's start with the hot water. Edna Hitchcock died, as far as the medical examiner can determine, on June 15 between the hours of ten A.M. and two P.M. The fact of the temperature of the water makes the determination a bit vague. You can imagine we would therefore be very interested in *why* someone would have filled the tub with hot water."

"Did someone hope to confuse the time of death with the hot water? You say it made the time of death more vague. Suppose someone had an alibi for only portions of the day. Say they had a—"

"At any rate, you would assume it made no sense for someone to remain in the house with a dead body and fiddle around with the bathwater

40

unless he or she were somehow involved in her death, don't you agree?''

Pete considered this and nodded.

"And you arrived at . . . seven?"

Pete frowned. "Yes." It struck him as ironic that he had been so worried about the chief worrying about Martha that he had never once considered his own position in all this. But Rita had just vouched for his day between ten and two, and the people on the list could surely give him alibis for those times; what happened at or just before seven, the hot water, could be of no significance if taken separate from what happened before . . .

Finally, the chief stood up. He fished around in his shirt pocket and pulled out a dog-eared card and wrote a phone number on its back. "Appreciate your help. If you think of anything else, I'd appreciate a call. Home number."

Pete took the card. The two men shook hands. The chief walked out, spoke in modulated tones to Rita for a few minutes, and left Factotum.

Pete leaned back in his chair and sighed.

Chapter
6

Every time Martha closed her eyes she saw the house at the Point. Every time she opened them she saw the bare bones of Hillerman's rafters. She lay on the bed, one of the few pieces of furniture Hillerman had provided, and tried to keep her eyes open. She pulled the comforter up around her ears, chilly in the unheated, uninsulated attic of the boat-house. It perched on the dune overlooking Close Harbor and had appealed to her basically forlorn nature, just as her mother's house had, once. Her mother's house sat on the very end of the island of Nashtoba, up on its own dune formation they called the Point. The house was as gray as the sky and water, and its three-sided open porch gave it all kinds of spidery shadows and weird impressions. When she had been a child there, other children had run up onto the porch on a dare to ring the bell. Martha sat upright. Hadn't one of the frequent ringers been Peter Bartholomew? She would have to go back to that house, some day. Soon. She was filled with the dread of it even as she thought of it. Just then her own door rattled with a knock.

This time she knew it was Bill Freed—knew it because of the hour, and because of the intensity of the knock—but still she wrapped herself in her blanket and went to the window to look. Yes, there was his ridiculously tiny little Rabbit next to her yellow VW, the two of them looking like Easter eggs. She went into the kitchen and, yes, there he was, hunkered down to peer in through the pane in the door.

"I left her," he said, and Martha stared at him. "I left Adrienne. It was all so foolish, Martha; I should have done it long ago. It's been pretty clear to me for so long: You're the best thing that ever happened to me. . . ."

It was too bad, thought Martha, that he continually talked like a walking soap. It was too bad that she couldn't be happy about this news. It was too bad that she only wanted him on loan, secret and safe and . . . yes, safe. But there it was, and here he was.

"Where are you staying?" she asked, and she knew before he answered that he was going to say "Here, of course."

The old truck bounced off the rutted road to pull in behind the yellow VW, and Pete's stomach did the same lurching thing it did when it discovered it was ten P.M. and he had forgotten to feed it. He should have eaten first, but after the chief had left, all Pete could think about was Martha, and what Hardy had told him, and he knew the chief would be speaking to her soon if he hadn't done so already, and Pete wanted to . . . wanted to what?

43

Warn her? Not really. He just wanted to . . . wanted to what?

He got out of the truck and walked along the path through the beach grass up to the stairs that ran along the outside wall to the top story of the boathouse. It was a nice spot, he thought, as he looked out from the stairs over the sand to Close Harbor and the Hook out beyond. It would be nice at night—lots of lights. He turned to face the door and found that he could look right into the kitchen through the small square panes of glass to see an old sink on legs, a hot plate, a half-size refrigerator, and open shelves with almost nothing on them. They weren't the shelves of someone who was planning to stick around. He knocked on the door and Martha appeared, wearing a man's wool shirt that was ripped at one shoulder, worn jeans, and the same pair of running shoes she had worn that day at Factotum. Her eyes were a deeper green today, and her hair wafted behind her like a contrail of a jet. The Ukrainian dancer in Pete's stomach up-tempoed.

"Come in," she said. It sounded nice, very nice. He followed her through the kitchen, into her living area, and looked around at the cot she was using for a couch, the barrel with the lamp on it that served for an end table, the one rocking chair, the remaining empty spaces. Through an archway he could see her bed and, above the bed, the windows and the water beyond. Beside the bed was an oak bureau, still separated from its drawers. She must have noticed him looking.

"Mice in the drawers," she said, and just then, from around the corner of the archway, there came a loud crash.

44

"You sure there's nothing larger than mice in there?" he asked, but instead of laughing, Martha looked worried.

She's got to loosen up more, crack a smile now and then, he thought. He opened his mouth to say something surefire witty, something that would bring the desired result, but behind him there was another knock on the door that rattled the panes, and they both turned to see Will McOwat and Paul Roose looking at them through the glass. It was difficult to say which of the four of them looked more surprised.

"I'm sorry to bother you, Ms. Hitchcock," said the chief.

"I'll shove off," said Pete, for the second time, aware that the irony of the situation was not lost on the chief himself. But Martha said, at once and slightly desperately, "No, please!"

Pete looked at her. She was staring at the chief.

"This won't take long. I'm sure it won't. I'd like you to stay. I have something to ask you. I don't mind you being here."

"It might be better . . ." began the chief, but Martha cut in, her voice suddenly not the pleasant thing it had once been.

"I said I'd prefer he stay."

Martha sat down on the cot.

Pete sat down beside her.

The chief sat in the rocker and leaned forward, while Paul Roose stood, still half in the kitchen and half out.

"Do you recall, Ms. Hitchcock, my asking you the other day about sleeping pills?" began the chief, and Pete felt an immediate sense of dread.

"No," said Martha.

45

"I asked you if you knew your mother was taking sleeping pills and you answered no. That's correct, Paul? She answered no?"

Paul Roose nodded. It seemed to Pete that he was aging before his eyes. His eyes were pouchy, his hair white and thin. The chief leaned forward even more, and his forehead creased all the way back into what had once been his hairline.

"And yet I find that on May 19 of this year, you brought a bottle of Seconal sleeping pills into Dr. Rogers's office and asked him several questions about their use and side effects. The bottle was a prescription he had written the month previous for your mother. You asked him to give your mother no more of that particular medication. He did not, by the way. When the cause of death was determined, Dr. Rogers took it upon himself to find out who did: A Dr. Brixton had written her a prescription that was filled in Bradford several days after he discontinued his own. Still, you can see this leaves us with several unanswered questions."

Pete coughed. Martha didn't move or speak. Pete wondered if etiquette dictated that now was the time to offer once again to leave. He leaned forward so that his weight was on the balls of his feet instead of on his butt and said, "Perhaps I . . ."

Martha laid a hand that was like a feather on his left thigh. Pete sat back down and didn't—couldn't have—moved again.

"One," continued the chief, "why did you lie to us?"

Martha didn't answer.

"And two, what did you do with that particular bottle, the bottle Rogers prescribed, the bottle that you took out of his office on May 19?"

Cripes, thought Pete, does he have to sound like Perry Mason?

Martha looked down at her hands and twisted them, and Pete felt something inside his chest twist likewise.

"I don't *think* I put them in my mother's drink," said Martha, and Pete snapped around to look at her.

The chief didn't change expression. "What *do* you think you did with them?"

Martha shrugged. "I think I threw them away. I was sleeping fine, myself."

Pete coughed. He was beginning to feel just the slightest bit sorry for the chief.

"You threw this prescription out where, Ms. Hitchcock?"

Martha shrugged again. "I can't remember."

The chief's voice, for the first time, became a decibel louder. "Our choices being?"

"The garbage. The wastebasket."

"Whose? Your own? Where?"

"I don't know. Boston, I think."

"You carried the pills from Nashtoba to Boston and then threw them out there?"

The telephone rang. Martha looked at the chief, her expression such a parody of submission that Pete wanted to laugh, and the chief waved her toward the phone. The phone was beside them on the barrel, and everyone in the room could hear her speaking.

"I said no."

47

Pause.

"No, you can't. I told you why."

Pause.

"I have other people staying here right now; there's no room for you, for one."

Pause.

"The police, to name a few."

The conversation ended abruptly. The chief stared hard at Pete, and Pete looked out the window. The sky was gray. Still.

"My dentist," said Martha, and she smiled at Paul Roose. Paul Roose looked away, something Pete took for a bad sign.

The chief fished a cigarette pack out of his jacket pocket, pulled out a cigarette, jammed it into his mouth, immediately removed it, and shoved it back into the pack. Pete could picture the soggy end of it sticking to the one next to it; later the chief would unstick them and put the now-crusty end back in his mouth. . . . Pete swallowed.

"And three," the chief went on, "you must have seen your mother at her house in May when you got the pills from her. You said you hadn't seen her for—"

"I saw the pills," said Martha. "I didn't see my mother."

"You walk around your mother's house at will when she's not home?"

Martha didn't answer.

"And four . . ."

Pete was getting pretty annoyed with all this counting.

"While we're speaking of your mother's house, the house was your mother's; most of the money

48

was your father's. He left an odd arrangement when he died—a nominal amount of money to your mother with the bulk to you, yet your mother didn't contest this. Why was that?"

Again Martha didn't speak. Pete was beginning to recognize this habit: ignoring things she hoped would go away.

"Why did your father do that, Ms. Hitchcock?"

"I guess you'll have to ask him," said Martha.

Pete coughed again, and the chief glared at him.

"You have no idea why your father did this?"

Martha sighed, a knuckling-under kind of sigh that Pete didn't believe for a minute. "It has nothing to do with my mother's death."

They all sat in silence for several seconds while the chief looked at his notebook. "What about your mother's will, Ms. Hitchcock? The will your mother wrote leaves everything to you—house, money. . . . Of course, I don't suppose you need the money, but there *is* the house. A quite valuable house, on the water, with all that land. . . ." He was looking at her without expression, just as Martha was looking back at him. Pete felt unequal to the match.

"Of course," continued the chief, "that was the first will your mother wrote; then there was the new one she was seeing the lawyer about on Wednesday."

Finally Martha's face cracked. She frowned. "What Wednesday?"

The chief stood up from the chair, and the rocker started rocking wildly—for the first time, Pete noticed. "Don't worry," said the chief. "Her appointment was for the Wednesday *after* she died. She never got it changed, officially. But you knew that, of course.''

"Of course," said Martha, and Pete wanted to shake her.

Now the chief was frowning as well. "Ms. Hitchcock, I'm sure you are aware that if you can't answer a few of these questions to our satisfaction we are going to be forced to—"

Martha stood up also. "I don't give a damn what you do."

After a pause, the chief's face broke into a wide grin. "I'm starting to get a kick out of you, Martha."

"Thanks, Willy."

He stopped smiling.

Pete stood up beside Martha and cleared his throat.

"Dr. Rogers also informs me you mentioned your mother's drinking to him in May. You remember me asking about your mother's drinking habits?"

"No, I don't," Martha snapped.

"And you forgot all about the bottle of pills— pills for a controlled substance that happens to be the same thing that killed your mother."

"Yes."

Silence. Pete looked at Paul Roose, who looked away.

"You really don't give a damn, do you?" asked the chief.

Martha didn't answer.

The chief looked at Pete as if for explanations, but Pete didn't have any—or at least the ones he had were his own and not applicable here.

After the police had gone, Pete turned to Martha. "Now look—" he began, but Martha gave him a look that shut him up fast.

"I think you'd better go after all," she said.

Against his better judgment, but not feeling that he had much other choice, he left.

Chapter

7

Pete was having another bad day. He used to love to come to Sarah Abrew's house each morning, loved the tiny half Cape that reminded him of his own cramped living quarters. Connie had told Pete once that she felt like a bull in a china shop at Sarah's, and Pete hadn't understood that at all. Connie was tall—five feet eight inches or so—but lean and graceful and surefooted. There was nothing in the way at Sarah's, and she didn't have a lot of knickknacks around that Connie would have been apt to break. Come to think of it, Connie hadn't much liked their own little cottage either. It was funny that only now would Pete remember some of her cracks and realize what he had taken at the time for jokes seemed to have had deeper meaning. Once he had been trying to find a dry place to store a cord of wood for a customer, and Connie had said, "Why don't you just stack it in the kitchen? We can eat off the television and do the dishes in the bathroom sink."

Pete pushed Connie out of his mind and looked

around Sarah's. Sarah had once been a seamstress, and the tools of her trade still spilled out all over her living room the same way that Pete's tools spilled out all over his. He sat on the couch and immediately picked up a pin and found pieces of flannel were adhering to his cuffs. He looked across the little room to where Sarah sat perched in a thronelike Victorian chair and sighed. She was frowning.

He used to love to see Sarah. He valued her opinion to the point that he had created what he secretly called the Sarah Abrew Test. Whenever he was trying to hire a new employee, as he was attempting to do now, he would ask himself "Would Sarah like him/her?" It used to work pretty well, overlooking for the minute that Connie had passed the Sarah Abrew Test with flying colors.

And that brought them back around to the matter at hand. He used to love to see Sarah, but today his head was full of the Hitchcocks and hers was . . . He slouched down further on a couch that he was beginning to suspect she had selected because it left the sitter's head a good four inches below her own, thought of the king of Siam, and tried not to listen.

"Why else do you think she came here, Peter, hm? Answer me that."

"I was trying to tell you about Martha, Sarah. I mean, about Edna. It was the temperature of the water, see, that made the whole thing—"

"Do you think she accidentally happened through here on her way someplace else?"

Pete looked at the tiny old woman. Her eyes were so bright behind watery lenses that he was

53

beginning to suspect she could read perfectly well. She had short, straight, snow-white hair that was standing up on spikes as if it were carrying the household current. "Do you want me to read this paper or not?"

"No, I don't want you to read me the paper. To listen to you, you'd think this place was disconnected from the whole country. Why don't they ever have real news? We could be at war with Russia and I'd never even know it. And I don't want to hear any more about the Hitchcock business, either. Connie is staying at the Whiteaker. How much do you think that's costing her, hm? You drive right by there, and it wouldn't kill you to be generous for once in your life. Hm?"

Pete decided to defend himself on all charges, in order. "Just because I read the news doesn't mean I wrote it. And if we were at war with Russia, it would probably be because you caused it. And I think what's happened to poor Martha Hitchcock is a lot more interesting than who's staying at the Whiteaker, which is not on my way home, and whose rates are not my fault. What do you want me to do, ask her if she'd like to move back in to save a few bucks?"

Something twitched at the corner of Sarah's mouth and gleamed in her eye. "Couldn't hurt to ask."

Pete tried, again, to divert the course of conversation back to Edna Hitchcock. "You knew the Hitchcocks, Sarah. Didn't you used to do some clothes for—"

Sarah reached for her cane and rapped it on the braided rug. "I'm talking about your wife." She rammed the cane one more time onto the floor, and it seemed to Pete that she leaned on it heavily and swayed. She closed her eyes. When her eyes were shut all the life went out of her, and she looked all of her eighty-six years. Pete felt a pang of something—not remorse but close to it. He got up, crossed the few feet to her chair, and knelt down in front of her with his hands on her knees. "Are you all right?"

Her eyes flashed open, and her hair seemed to crackle. She raised her cane, and Pete leaned back. "Get the foolish paper and read it to me, then. Even Pfiefer's chickens have got to be better than this."

Pete moved back to the couch, picked up the paper, and looked at her. She still didn't look quite right.

"Read the paper! What am I paying you for?"

Paying me, thought Pete. Twenty years before when he had agreed to do this for five dollars a week he had never dreamed that he'd still be here twenty years later and it taking an hour and a half each day to do it. . . . But that wasn't fair. She had tried to give him more money many times, and he had tried to do it for nothing as many times back. And it had been mutually agreeable, this hour and a half each morning, until she started in on all this stuff about Connie.

"She came to see me," said Sarah, the minute Pete had snapped open the paper to the first news-worthy thing he could find that had nothing to do with Russia or chickens.

"Martha?"

"Martha! God help me if I hear another word about Martha. Your wife came to see me. Remember her, your wife?"

"No," said Pete, "I don't." And he began to read.

The situation back at the office was only a slight improvement over the one at Sarah's. It was Rita's turn, this time, and although her subject wasn't Connie, it was just as bad. It was almost summer. They had not yet hired the additional help. If Pete would just sit down for ten minutes and help her write up an ad . . . And Rita felt they should design an employment application like real companies did. Factotum was an unusual place and its employees were required to have unusual skills. You had to get along with people, it was most helpful if you were capable of doing hard physical work, but you still had to handle things that took more finesse. John Peary had stopped in; John Peary, Pete knew, would never pass the Sarah Abrew Test.

"I'll tell you what," said Pete, after long discussion. "You do the ad and the application. When you get them back you make first cuts, then I'll go through them and make second cuts. Then we'll sit down with whoever is left. How's that?"

"Fine," said Rita. When Rita said "fine," it usually didn't mean "fine" at all. Whenever Rita said "fine," Pete knew it just meant it would be a few hours before he found out what was really unfine about it. When Rita said "fine," it was usually time for Pete to remember all the smart things Rita had done for Factotum, all the right things she had done for him, such as remaining handy and silent when she found out Connie had left, and later on, when Pete divorced her . . . Darn it, thought Pete, wasn't there one minute out of every day when he didn't have to start thinking about her? What he needed was a distraction. Someone else. For a whole year now he had been unable to take that next step back out into the single world, and it was time he did so.

When the phone rang Pete reached past Rita's manicured fingers to pick it up—it was, at the moment, the most convenient distraction he could find—and when he heard Martha Hitchcock's voice on the other end he was pleasantly surprised at the extent to which he did suddenly feel distracted. Very distracted. He waited for Martha to speak again. She had that kind of voice that, once you heard it, you wanted to hear it again soon; that kind of voice. In listening to the sound of it he lost track of the actual words for a minute, and it took him a few more to realize she was talking to him about his job.

"A business proposition," she was saying. "If you have a minute, I could stop by to discuss it."

"Lunch," said Pete, for no particular reason except that once again his stomach was doing that odd kind of thrumming and he realized it must be that time, but then he repeated it. "We could have lunch," he said. And despite Rita's looking at him sideways with a don't-mind-about-me kind of look, he added, "Rita and I were about to head for Lupo's. Would you like to join us and we could discuss it there?" Lunch with Rita was a pretty standard deal, and besides, they were partners, and what was business for Pete was also business for Rita. And besides, with Rita along nobody would be fool enough to think it was really a date or something.

Martha Hitchcock seemed to take a long time to

say it, but finally she said it. "All right," she said. "I'll meet you there."

Pete's stomach was now doing Fred Astaire–type moves up the side wall into his chest. I must be starving, he thought.

Lupo's was Pete and Rita's favorite. The table-cloths were red and white and real cotton, the booths were roomy, and the menu was a black-board containing ten of the best things Pete could ever hope to eat on any one given day. The place sat 200 yards from the water, but so did everything on Nashtoba; the view was secondary to the per-fect, simple food and the coldness of the beer. Rita, announcing that she planned to eat and drink to excess, ordered the chicken-salad plate and a glass of white wine. Pete and Martha ordered ham-burgers; Pete ordered a beer, since Rita started it, and Martha ordered a daiquiri. A daiquiri for lunch was big time to Pete, but then Connie was the only woman Pete had ever met who drank nothing but beer.

Martha wasted no time. Long before the food arrived, she handed Pete the original copy of the letter the chief had shown Pete in his office. Pete handed it to Rita and looked at it with her as she read it.

"It's my aunt," said Martha. "She's dead, and I want to find out if she had this baby. I think she did, since it says here it was too late to do anything else, but the funny part is that she didn't marry. I'm sure she didn't, and I have no known cousin. Factotum did that genealogy for the Bradfords."

And how did she know that? Pete wondered.

"And I thought this might be the same kind of

work. Would you do it? Try to track this baby down?" She looked from Pete to Rita. Pete and Rita looked at each other and then looked back.

"A lot can happen," said Rita. "There very well might not be a baby at all."

"I know that," said Martha, sounding terse. Too terse. "And if there isn't a baby I need to know that too; that's all."

"Why?"

Pete looked at Rita.

Martha looked at both of them, one at a time, again. Her hair was down this time, and it was the usual Nashtoba-in-June cold—she wore a heavy sweater and tight jeans. She looked great.

"There's no one else," she said.

Pete cleared his throat. "I certainly think we can handle this, don't you, Rita?"

Rita gave him a look with one eyebrow raised and said, "Up to you."

Pete frowned at her. "Up to you" never meant "up to you," either; "up to you" usually meant "if you want to make this huge mistake, then you do it on your own"; that kind of thing. "Up to you" was even more irritating to Pete than "fine": It reminded Pete of his mother, and it was for that reason, among the others that Pete was just beginning to consider that day, that he turned to Martha and said, "You're on."

Then it happened. He looked at Martha, and behind her through the window he saw the tall woman with the pale brown hair. He stood up. "Rita . . ."

"What?"

He reached into his wallet and flung two twenties down onto the table, although he and Rita usually went Dutch. "I have to go. Can you drop her at Factotum, Martha?"

Then he hung a left at the kitchen door and bolted through it out the back.

Rita looked at the vanishing form of Peter Bartholomew and then at the pale face of Martha Hitchcock and decided to go find him in the kitchen and kill him. *Honestly!*

"He's hiding from his wife," said Rita. "Exwife," she corrected herself. "She ran off with Glen Newcomb, who used to work here. You know him?"

Martha shook her head.

"Well, now she's back alone and I don't need to tell you she's got the whole island buzzing. Do you know her? Connie?"

Martha shook her head again and looked at the door with the look of the hunted.

And *you* have the whole island buzzing, thought Rita. Did you or didn't you kill your mother? Rita looked at her, and there on the spot she decided that she didn't trust her. She certainly looked miserable, but that could just be because her mother was dead. No matter how rotten your relationship, or maybe the more rotten your relationship, you had a really tough time of it when your mother died. Rita thought momentarily of Maxine and narrowed her eyes. The little creep will go paint the town red when I kick the bucket, she thought. Just then she caught the form of Connie out of the corner of her eye as she approached their booth and did what she hoped was a convincing double take.

"Connie! How nice to see you!"

Connie was in leather jacket and jeans and she

wore huaraches over socks on her feet. She leaned down and rested an arm on Rita's shoulder.

"Hey, Rita." She looked at Martha, and her face became puzzled. "Isn't Pete . . ."

As she spoke, Pete's truck roared to life in the parking lot and wheeled away. An expression of pain flashed across Connie's face and then she turned, admirably regrouping her facial muscles to smile at Martha. "Hi," she said. Just that.

"Hi."

Martha said, "Hi," back.

"Pete had to run," said Rita. "Won't you sit down? This is Martha Hitchcock. Do you know Martha? This is Connie Bartholo . . . Connie . . ."

"Still Bartholomew," said Connie. She looked back toward the parking lot. "I suppose it's time I did something about that. Thanks, no, I gotta go. Just wanted to say hi to . . . just wanted to say hi. How is . . . everything?"

"Fine!" said Rita. "Fine!" *God,* she hated the way she said that word. The things that she heard coming out of her own mouth sometimes . . . "Very busy," she amended. "I'll tell Pete I saw you. I will." That sounded neutral enough.

Connie studied Rita's face for a second and then lifted long fingers in a wave and moved off without another word, her dark green TR-6 spurting out of the lot shortly afterward, but in the opposite direction from the one Pete had taken.

Rita wrapped her shell-pink oval nails around the stem of the sweating wineglass and raised it to her lips, noticing with absentminded pleasure that the half moon of lipstick she left on the glass was indeed the exact color of her nails. And what else do I have to do lately, she thought, except spend all night polishing my nails and shopping for lipstick and worrying about Maxine and Pete? Rita was beginning to feel slightly panic-stricken about her life.

She gave Martha another look. Martha's face wore the expression of a person who was not in the place she wanted to be and not with the person of her choice. Rita began to mull that over. As soon as the food arrived, she wolfed through it so that Martha could get on with whatever she wanted to get on with. Whenever she was nervous she talked too much, and this time was no exception: Rita heard herself rambling on between mouthfuls about Factotum and Pete and Connie and Maxine and God knew what else. Martha didn't help much. When they were finally back out in Martha's car, she breathed a sigh of relief. It was almost over.

She breathed too soon.

They hadn't even moved anywhere—Rita wasn't even sure if the car were actually turned on—when she felt a shock shoot through her from her feet to her ears and heard a sound that sounded like *Poogh!* That was *just* what it sounded like: *Poogh!* She turned around, and there was a car the color and luster of wet seaweed fornicating with the rear of the VW bug. Rita wanted to cry. She didn't need this, she really didn't. She was going to *kill* Pete, she really was. I mean really, how juvenile! And poor Martha! Who didn't need this more than Martha didn't? Rita was about to say something she had first learned from Maxine several months before when around to Martha's window came a man, and anything Rita had been thinking about him died away unsaid.

"I can't tell you how sorry I am," he said. "I only just this morning arrived in this beautiful place, and I'm afraid I was distracted by the scenery. I know it's no excuse. Are you both all right?"

His name was John Clark. He was tall and slim and had that Cary Grant type of gray hair that Rita had always been particularly fond of. He wore a gray suit that showed it off very nicely and a pink shirt. *Pink.* You didn't see things like this on Nashtoba. He was older than Rita—midfifties, perhaps—but definitely not *too* old: Rita had just turned forty-two and was feeling it. John Clark kept smiling at her.

"We hardly felt it," said Rita. "It was the smallest possible bump. I bet there's nothing wrong with the car, even."

That seemed to wake Martha up. She got out of the car, and Rita followed her, and the three of them walked around both vehicles, looking for dents. John Clark's car was an Audi. Rita sighed. If there was anything she loved more than an Audi . . . She snapped herself back to the business at hand. "Are you all right, Martha?"

Martha nodded.

"And I'm all right," said Rita. "And the cars are all right. But I suppose we should call the police just to be on the safe—"

"No," said Martha, quickly. "There's no need to do that. Everything is all right."

"Well, in that case," said John Clark, "might I suggest that we return inside and I will buy you ladies a drink?"

You didn't hear things like that on Nashtoba, either. Might I suggest! And before Rita knew quite what she was doing or why, she said, "I'd like that," and both Martha Hitchcock and she herself looked immediately and equally surprised.

"I have to be someplace," said Martha, and at once Rita said that was quite all right, but Mr. John Clark indicated that the offer was still open. He would be happy to drive her back to wherever she needed to be afterward.

What in all the world has gotten into me? Rita asked herself as she preceded her new companion back inside.

But whatever it was, she decided she liked it!

Chapter
8

The boathouse seemed to Pete to be almost colder inside than it was out. Martha had a quartz heater propped up in the corner, but she must have been participating in some kind of Puritan austerity program: It wasn't on, and instead, she was walking around in a man's flannel shirt over a sweater and again the blue jeans, with thick wool socks on her feet. She seemed to have an endless supply of men's old clothes lying around, he thought.

"I'm sorry about lunch," said Pete right away. "I don't know what . . ."

Martha held up both hands, flat. "Please." She closed her eyes briefly and reopened them. "I understand if you don't want to do this. You might not want to mix up with me much, I understand that. I . . ."

"Why not? Why wouldn't I want to mix up with you much?"

"They think I did it," she said, and her green eyes watched him.

Pete cleared his throat. "I did a job for a Republi-

65

can once," he said. "There's not much turning back after that."

She *almost* smiled. It wasn't going to be plain sailing, this smiling bit.

They sat down side by side on the cot and Pete began talking, and as he talked he could feel her body react as if it were taking a charge. "I thought we should discuss how to go about this thing first," he began, and he laid a yellow legal pad across his knees. "Of course, the first thing I need to know is anything you can remember about your family, your aunt Lizzie. . . ." All of a sudden, Pete remembered exactly how it was that he and his sister Polly had come to give The Spookhouse its name. It was where Lizzie had lived and drowned. The boat washed up on the rocks and she had been curled up in it, dead, the boat swamped, full of water. She had drowned, but in the boat, not out of it! The story got told and told, the house and the rocks pointed at over and over again, and The Spookhouse was born. "Anything you can remember," he went on, his voice feeling eerily hollow.

"I don't remember anything. I can't even find a picture of her. I don't know what we can do."

Easy, Pete wanted to say; don't panic, he wanted to say. "Well, in that case," he said, "we start looking for records. I'll get all the old records from the town hall. Births, deaths. If the baby were stillborn or—"

Martha closed her hand over her mouth.

"Of course, if Lizzie had the baby and gave it up for adoption, there wouldn't be anything there in the town hall; they amend all the birth certificates at the time of adoption in this state. All we would find would be anything that was filed under her adoptive name, and if we knew that, of course, we wouldn't need the town hall, would we?"

Pete smiled at Martha.

Martha didn't smile back.

"Still, I'd check all that out. And of course I'll talk to Hardy Rogers. He's been here long enough; he might know plenty, and since the parties are all . . . deceased . . . he might not mind talking. You could sign a paper giving permission as the only living relative. And there's this place outside of Boston called Rematch. You register there if you're looking for either your natural parents or a child you gave up, and they try to match people there. It's a long shot that the kid would even be around here, or have registered, or that they'd accept a registration from you as a cousin; I don't know, but I'd like to have us try it. Now let's see, the Korean War—1950, wasn't it? To '53 or so? So the kid would have been born somewhere in there. This Hal having been a serviceman in the Korean War, I wonder if there might be a way of tracking him down through the service. Be nice if we had a last name and the envelope to that letter. When you go back to the house maybe you could . . ."

Beside him, Martha stiffened.

"And of course there are the neighbors."

"Neighbors?" asked Martha.

"People out around the Point. A couple of the old-timers out there might know something about Lizzie being pregnant. And then we could talk to your family lawyer. Maybe some private adoption was arranged."

"Roberta Ballantine," said Martha. "But she's too young, I think. It was too long ago."

"Well, if all else fails there's always Beston's Porch."

And finally—finally—she smiled.

"So!" said Pete. "Keeping in mind there might very likely not have been a baby at all, does this seem like a good plan of action to start?"

Martha stood up and sat back down. She reached out a hand to the legal pad, drew it back, and stood up again. "I know there was a baby," she said.

Pete cleared his throat.

"I mean this. Really. I know there is. I could never explain it to you. I could never explain it to anyone." She was pacing away from him and was halfway across the living room now. She seemed to do better, speak less jerkily, from farther away.

"All my life," she began, turning from some distance and looking at him hard, apparently seeing or not seeing something that spurred her on, "all my life the one thing that has upset my mother most is what other people think. She once told me my reputation was the only thing I had—the *only* thing. What someone else, what some . . . *idiot* thinks about me is all that I am, nothing more." She crossed back to the cot fast and sat down next to Pete. Their knees jolted together. "I think it could be true, this baby. I'm sure if Lizzie had a baby they would hush it up, get rid of it, do anything. My mother was a chip off my grandmother's block, and if the two of them ganged up on poor Lizzie she wouldn't have stood a chance. Suppose this Hal were killed in the war? That's the most logical thing, isn't it really? He never came home,

68

and she was stuck here with her mother, her father, her sister, and a pregnancy. . . ." Martha stopped talking. She grabbed onto the one hand that she had been waving and held it fast with the other and looked away from Pete. "I'd like you to look. I think your plan is . . . perfect. I had no idea you could come up with a plan like that."

Pete considered whether this was a compliment or an insult and decided it was best not to decide. "You'll have to help," he said. "The neighbors, for one—" He was stopped midsentence by the look of alarm on her face. She stood up and strode away again. She shook her head.

"I can't talk to those people. Please. I can't. I'm not . . . popular here." She tried to laugh but didn't quite make it. An ugly, squawking sound snuck out.

"That's all right. I can do the talking. You have to help with the list of who I talk to, that's all." To whom I talk? "When you make your notes of everything you remember, just add on some likely sources of information at the Point."

Martha had already jumped out of the room. When she returned some minutes later, she had a folded piece of paper in one hand and a checkbook in the other. "Here." She handed him the paper. "And I want to pay you, however much you feel you need to get started."

Pete shook his head and waved a hand at the checkbook. "No way. Let me see how far this all goes first."

Martha shook *her* head and waved her checkbook back at him. "No. I don't like to owe." She sat down beside him and began writing. She ripped

69

off the check and handed it to him. A thousand dollars.

"No," said Pete again, but she had taken hold of his arm and he was losing sight of the problem at hand. It's been way too long, he was thinking, as she leaned into him with her shoulder and shoved the check into his pocket.

"My auto mechanic charges me twenty-five dollars an hour," she said. "This adds up to only forty hours of work. There's at least forty hours of ideas on that pad of paper there, I'm sure. Take it, please."

She was still leaning into him, her thigh up against his and something that was definitely not a shoulder pressing into his side. He took the check. He leaned in. "Martha . . ."

She backed up.

"Thank you," she said.

"Thank *you*," said Pete.

As he got into his truck, it occurred to him that if all else failed he could always go back to school and become an auto mechanic.

When Pete returned to Factotum he was concerned to see that Rita was not yet back from lunch. Her chair was empty and there was no note; and if she had come back and gone out again she would have picked up the messages on the answering machine and she would have left Pete a note—Rita was very big on notes. Long, detailed notes. There was no note. Pete considered for a minute what it would mean if he had just seen Martha already returned from lunch while Rita was not yet back. Was she still there? With Connie? Hadn't Rita mentioned that she planned to eat and drink to excess? But to Rita, as Pete well knew, the "excess" was the one glass of wine and the plate of cold chicken. So where was she? Ah, there was the car now. Pete moved back to the door, hoping to see Rita, afraid she might be with Connie, peering surreptitiously out the window first. It was not a TR-6 out there; it was an Audi. A tall, city type was unfolding himself from behind the wheel and actually opening Rita's door for her. He was lifting up her hand! Cripes, don't tell me he's going to kiss it! He didn't kiss it. He sort of . . . saluted it, which was bad enough.

Rita jounced in, acting very flustered—more flustered than one glass of white wine could account for—and she had the strange man in tow. She was actually giggling. Pete frowned.

"Pete, I'd like you to meet John Clark."

Another giggle. John Clark shook Pete's hand and held it too long, and Pete decided he didn't like him. He looked . . . married.

"We met at Lupo's just now; he just arrived today from Connecticut—he's thinking of spending the summer. We had a small car accident and he offered to drive me home."

"An accident! In Martha's car? She didn't mention this to me!"

Now Rita frowned, at him. "Martha's all right. Her car is all right. She had to go, and I stayed for another drink. To settle my nerves, that's all." Rita began to busy herself behind the desk. "And what are you going to do this afternoon?" she asked him smiling.

Pete decided on the spot that anything would do. He was not going to sit around Factotum all afternoon and watch Rita . . . *smiling*. "Town

71

hall," he said. "The job for Martha." Well, at least that erased the goofy expression. She seemed to be thinking.

"Good," she said. "I'm glad you're doing it. I like that." Somehow that "good" didn't make him feel much better than "fine."

Myra Totobush was the clerk at the town hall. Pete and Myra knew each other: Myra knew that Pete wouldn't be asking for records on the Denault family unless he had a good reason, and Pete knew Myra would have whatever his reason was all over Nashtoba before the engine in his truck warmed up. He decided to tell her it was another genealogy: A genealogy sounded a lot better—or at least Pete thought Myra would think it would—than the real story about the baby. Myra promised him she would start looking as soon as she could. Pete tried to narrow her down, but the more he tried to narrow her down the wider the time span became and the more off the subject she got. Did Pete know that Myra's own genealogy was quite interesting? That Myra's Uncle Harmon was a descendant of Ethan Allen? Pete didn't, and Myra was shocked. It might take her a week to find the information he was requesting. Everyone on Nashtoba knew about her Uncle Harmon: They had wanted her to ride in the Fourth of July Parade because of it, but Myra wasn't going to share any car with Leona Beggs. Leona was only descended from some old pilgrim whose name Myra couldn't remember; and that same pilgrim Myra couldn't remember lived out of wedlock with some Indian, and that was what Leona Beggs was descended from. It seemed clear to Pete that if he helped Myra knock Leona

Beggs he could reduce the time it would take Myra to do the job from one week to one day, but Pete didn't want to knock Leona. If the pilgrim and the Indian wanted to live together, Pete figured Ethan Allen and Uncle Harmon and Myra Totobush ought to have let them. And the longer it took her to do her part of the job, the longer it would take Pete to do his, and the longer this job took him the more he would get to see of Martha. Pete walked out to his truck and sat there for a few seconds without starting it. He wanted to see Martha. It felt nice.

Chapter
9

Martha's bare feet were cold, and the wind seemed to run up inside her sweatshirt and out at the wrists, taking all her body heat with it. She stepped up her pace, pushing off into the sand firmly, aware of the pull all the way up the backs of her legs. Keep moving. Before she knew it she was at the dock, and the lights of the Whiteaker were melting in stringy pools out over the water. She had always loved the Whiteaker, and she gave a minute's thought to crossing its wide veranda and entering the bar and ordering a daiquiri—not the frozen kind, all full of slush, but the plain rum and lime juice over ice that always looked like the tide over the bars when it was low. She vaulted up onto the dock and stopped there. She had told Bill the dock for a reason, and the dock it would be. She walked out to the end, leaned against the left-hand piling, and looked back at the hotel. A woman was leaning on the rail, looking across the harbor to the lights of the Hook. Connie Bartholo-mew. Of course she would be staying at the Whiteaker—everyone stayed at the Whiteaker; it was either the Whiteaker or Mooney's guest house, with the bathroom down the hall and the obligatory tell-us-everything-about-your-life breakfast in the dining room.

Martha leaned farther back into the shadow of the pilings and watched Connie Bartholomew. She was smoking a cigarette, leaning out over the sand, the collar of her leather jacket turned up and her backside projecting toward the hotel lobby. Martha watched a tall, slim shape come down the steps and give a long, slow glance at the back end of Connie. John Clark. Of course he would be staying there also. He stopped and spoke to Connie and moved on around toward the parking lot behind the hotel. To see Rita? Martha sat down on the dock and swung her legs to keep warm and started thinking about things that seemed to begin with Rita Peck and John Clark and end up with Connie and Peter Bartholomew, skimming over on the way a few musings about Glen Newcomb and Adrienne and Bill. She wondered what Adrienne was doing now. Suddenly Martha remembered a recent phone fight with her mother, Bill in the background trying to interject a calming influence, her mother asking who that voice was, and Martha's pride in the cleverness of her response: "Just another married man."

There was Bill, coming down the steps of the Whiteaker, not giving Connie Bartholomew a single glance. Martha stood up. He saw her, and even from the end of the dock Martha could see him lighten up, see him raise his head to her, jump over the last three porch steps and hit the dock loping. Then it happened—that same old warning bell: the tightness in her chest, the tingling in her fingers, the rapid breathing and the dizziness, the seeing black spots. What if he started in again about wanting to live with her? He was there, in front of her. He was grabbing her, sliding his hands up under her sweatshirt and sucking at her mouth. She tried to push him away.

"Bill," she said, "we have to stop meeting like this."

Connie Bartholomew drove to Sarah's the next morning, keeping a cautious look out for Pete's blue truck. She wasn't one to sneak around. If there was one thing Connie wasn't, it was a sneak; but she also wasn't a total fool. It didn't take three people at a lunch table turning into two and an old Jeep truck tearing out of the lot for it to dawn bright as day that her exhusband didn't want to see her. So why didn't he just tell her, dammit! It was no big skin off her nose. And why didn't Rita stop making excuses and just say right out he didn't want to see her? Damned Rita. Connie had always suspected that Rita had a thing for Pete, old lady though she was; and that Pete, if he weren't such a goody-two-shoes-stick-in-the-mud, would open his eyes one of these days and see he was kind of nuts about her too. At least it seemed to Connie that he *should* be kind of nuts about her: There they were, day after day, in that same old sardine can of an office, each one of them trying to out-nice the other. . . . Certain things made perfect sense in this life, thought Connie. What didn't make perfect sense was why she had ever come back here, why *she* should feel so hurt when she was the one who had left. But what else could she have done? When Glen and she had gotten popped that one day—not that she was blaming the booze; she wasn't about to do that. You didn't do drunk what you didn't want to do sober. She had gotten back at Pete for nothing he'd ever done to her, and then she had upped and left. That had been all her idea—poor Glen had been dragged off the island by the hair of his head, just about—but after that day with Glen she hadn't wanted to see Pete. She wasn't a liar—she would have told him right out—but she wouldn't have been able to stand one minute looking into his big brown eyes. Which would have been worse? Watching those eyes hate her or watching them forgive her? God! And now when it seemed like he wasn't doing either, wasn't even interested, why should that hurt? Why? The hell with him, thought Connie. It was his fault too. He wasn't able to hear her, or something—wasn't able to get a read on her panic at the thought of life in that cottage, at life on Nashtoba, every day the same as the one before, each one plodding by until she was old like her mother. . . . Like her mother. Connie couldn't have been less like her mother if she had set out purposely with that end in mind. Her parents were both short, retiring, moody people; but still, she knew well all the little habits she shared with her mother, little habits that she found, in her mother, to be most annoying and that seemed to crop up when she least wanted to hear about them in herself. But Pete had never minded her little foibles—or he hadn't seemed to mind.

Connie shook her head. Pete didn't want to see her, and that was that. She looked at her watch. Ten-thirty. Pete would surely have left Sarah's by now, and the coast would be clear. Sarah. Now there was someone on her side. Not that there were sides, really; not that she even cared who thought what or whether her parents ever for one day of their lives could understand the way she thought or who she was or . . . It was odd, really, to think how much that had all once mattered to her, how much Pete had mattered to her, how much fun it had all been. She remembered one day in particular when they never got out of bed. . . . Connie started to laugh to herself, then very abruptly stopped laughing. She had always figured that somewhere in there they would at least have tried to talk things out, but then the letter from his lawyer had arrived and that was that. She'd been sure he filed so fast because there was someone else, but Sarah said no, no one. But still, Sarah was acting very strange about this Hitchcock woman, this Martha; not that Connie blamed her. The Hitchcocks were snobs, the whole bunch of them—Edna the worst, of course, but the daughter a close second. And now Edna was dead. . . . Connie didn't want to think about that any more. She pulled into Sarah's drive and hopped out of the car without opening the door. Now this car was another thing, another case in point. Could she ever on her best day see Pete buying a car like this Triumph? Convertible? Oh, she could hear him now—how the roof would leak in winter (okay, it did leak a little), how cold it would be (in winter, maybe, but oh to drive around in the summer with the top down!)—and Lord, she was sick of that old truck. And he kept fixing it, explaining to her over and over again that he was *attached* to it! He was attached to everything. That house, that marsh, that secret place on the Point they used to go parking in, that truck, and just about anyone he'd ever met for a single minute in his whole life. Except for her, of course. Still, she had been glad when she had finally seen that old truck parked in front of Lupo's—why *was* that? Because it proved her right: The man was incapable of change, and she was right to leave him.

Connie shoved open Sarah's door and hollered out to her as she went, then grabbed her by her thin shoulders and gave her a huge hug when she appeared. She sank down onto Sarah's couch and hung her feet over the arm, all ready for a long listen. It was nice, she thought, to come here. It was nice—she had to admit it—that *some* things never changed.

Chapter
10

There were plenty of things Pete could be doing, but what he wanted to do now was talk to Hardy, again. Pete was worried about Martha, and so, it turned out, was Hardy. But since Pete's excuse to be calling again was supposed to be Lizzie's baby, they both pretended for some time that that was the only reason he had come. Pete explained about his job with Martha and asked Hardy if he had taken care of the Hitchcock family.

"I took care of Lizzie and Edna, yes, if that's what you mean," Hardy answered, his blue eyes flickering oddly.

"And Martha?"

"And Martha, after a while."

"After a while?"

Hardy Rogers stared at Pete for what seemed like a full minute, counting it out in the old "one Mississippi, two Mississippi" fashion, and seemed to come to some sort of conclusion that brought him up more vertically in his chair and smoothed his eyebrows back down to mere bushy vines.

"Yes, Lizzie was pregnant. I saw her and told her she was—as if she didn't already know it herself by then—and I told her to go home and tell her father and mother and if they booted her out to come back here and I'd find her a place to go. That was the last time I saw Lizzie professionally. Alive. And the last time I saw the rest of 'em until Martha was about six or so. They came back to me with her one night around midnight when she was delirious with fever. Scared them to death. They'd been seeing Brixton up in Bradford—as if I were the one who got Lizzie pregnant! Jesus Christ! Edna and Frank and Martha came back to me after that, till Edna got pissed again and went to Brixton. He's the one who gave her the last Seconal."

And there they were, back onto the subject of the Seconal.

"But if Edna had Seconal anyway, why do they care about Martha's . . ."

Hardy tipped back in the chair and rubbed his hands over his face. He looked out the window past Pete's head for another eternal minute and then clapped his eyes back onto Pete's. "Because of you. They need to tie someone else in. Even if Edna took her own pills, she still didn't fill up her tub with hot water after she did it."

They looked at each other in silence, until Pete started jiggling his foot. "May is a whole month ago," he said.

"So what." Hardy stood up, and Pete thought, looking at his back, how funny it was that the whole island called him Hardy behind his back, but he had never heard anyone dare to do it to his face.

"Dr. Rogers," Pete began again, "about Lizzie's baby: You don't know if she ever actually gave birth?"

"She gave birth all right," he said, and Pete leaned forward as Hardy sat back down. "Leastways that's what the autopsy showed."

"When? When did she give birth?"

"Christ almighty! How the hell should I know that?" Hardy stood up again, and this time he seemed to mean it. He walked toward the door. "If you want to help Martha, you have better ways of doing it than worrying about some baby. You tell her that the fat-ass cop is no joke. You tell her that, will you?"

"I will," said Pete. He followed Hardy into the hall, and as Pete moved up next to him the doctor's eyes narrowed onto his forearm, where he had rolled up his sleeve.

"I thought I told you to keep that elbow strapped!"

"It's fine," said Pete, hastily bending it back and forth. Hardy retreated farther down the hall before Pete, and as he went Pete could hear a dull rumbling, out of which he was able to pick only the one word, "retire."

Pete kept calling Martha, but no one was ever home. Where could she have gone? He was pent up and anxious to tell her that at least he now knew that Lizzie had had a baby, had given birth. He was also anxious to reason with her about her behavior with the police, more so now that Hardy himself seemed to think there was some real danger.

He walked out into the kitchen and onto his

porch and looked out at the streak of gray on the horizon beyond the marsh, the last of the day's sun. He looked sideways at the porch chairs, but it was no fun sitting on the porch any more, and he didn't know quite why that was. As a matter of fact, it wasn't a whole lot of fun being in his house any more. He stepped off the porch onto the lawn and around the side of the house to his truck. He got in and started it up. So where was he going? He pulled out onto Shore Road and drove without thinking until he was across from the rutted road to Hillerman's. He turned down it. Yes, her car was there, but all the lights were out and it was too early for that. He sat in the truck, thinking. He wasn't about to go knocking on her door with the lights out like that: Maybe she was sick. He turned off the engine, got out of the truck, walked straight past Martha's stairs and down onto the beach. Not far in the distance he could see a figure walking away from him, head down, arms swinging. It was too dark to identify anything but a medium height and a slender shape, but still, he knew it was her. It stopped. It looked out at the Hook. It turned around and started back in his direction, and all of a sudden Pete felt he was wrong to be there, that he would be an intruder to her now. He stood still for only a minute, then he turned and went back to his truck and drove away.

The next morning Pete had lost all the steam that had carried him around like a nut the night before. He tried Martha once by phone but once only, and when there was still no answer he sat down with his legal pad and attempted to plan things out in a logical order. He had Martha's meager summation of the neighbors at the Point, but somehow he just wasn't up to the Point quite yet—it was too much Spookhouse, too much dead-women-in-tubs. Then there was the lawyer, of course, and Rematch, but it seemed best to wait on all that until the news from the town hall was in. So what did that leave him? It seemed to boil down to either Jean's windows, or Beston's porch, and Pete chose Beston's. Geographically if not metaphysically, it was the center of things, and it was also about as far from The Spookhouse as he could hope to get and still remain on this particular job.

Bert Barker was the first one of the group on Beston's porch to see him approaching. "Here he comes!" called Bert. "Four years of college experience right down the drain!"

Pete's smile was forced. Bert Barker had been saying that for fourteen years, and around year thirteen it had started to get on Pete's nerves. Of course it was around year thirteen that a lot of things started to get on Pete's nerves: Connie's defection, for example, and the now defunct Glen Newcomb. The Bert Barker College Speech actually seemed to have made some sense around year thirteen, when Pete was spending a lot of time charting his mistakes.

"How many years you been sittin' on this bench now, Bert?" asked Pete, aware that once he hit the bare, worn floorboards of Beston's he started talking like the old men who lived there, dropping the contracted ends to words, leaving off the *g*'s. Ed Healey threw back his head and sprayed a huge laugh up into the air. Pete watched his glutinous chins shiver with laughter; the four rolls of his belly shimmied. Ed Healey was an alcoholic, but the benign kind: He didn't drive or beat up his wife or do much of anything but sit around Beston's. He could have been sixty or seventy or older, but his face was so soft and fat and free of lines it was hard to tell. Or was it that he was free of the worries that gave people the lines in the first place? Beside Ed—or as beside Ed as another body could get, which put him just about to the other side of the bench—sat Evan Spender. Evan was easier to date—late fifties, really only just old enough for the porch at all—and Evan was still working as a repairman for the phone company; Pete always wondered whose phone was dead and waiting each time he drove by Beston's and saw Evan on the porch. On the other side of the porch, on an old metal chair next to the Coke machine, sat Bert Barker. Bert Barker lived off a prime piece of rental property over on the Hook that he had inherited with his wife, and he hadn't worked since he was forty-two. Of the three men, Pete knew that Evan Spender was going to be his best bet: He would have been more contemporary with Lizzie; he was out and around, repairing phones and talking to people; he also knew more than he let on—unlike the other two, who tended to let on more than they knew. Pete cocked an eyebrow at Evan, so that after he'd put his twenty-five cents into the machine and pulled out his tall bottle of cold Coke, Evan moved over enough so there was room on the bench for Pete. Pete took a long pull at his bottle and waited, not speaking.

"Christ, Pete, you guys are gettin' slow in yer old age. Why don't ya hire some decent help? You were s'posed to send Bill over Monday to fix my fence, and he still hasn't showed. Not like ya, know that?" This was from Bert Barker. Pete didn't want to talk fences, and he didn't much want to talk to Bert. There wasn't a mean bone in the other two, but Bert . . .

"We're shorthanded, Bert. Want a job?"

Ed Healey brayed again, and Evan smiled down at a spot between his shoes. Bert Barker pursed his lips.

"Course, if ya spend all yer time diggin' round in the dirt 'bout the Denault family . . ."

So Myra had worked fast.

"What's this 'bout the Denaults, anyway?" asked Evan.

Pete had been right: It was going to be Evan who would zero him in on target.

"Yeah," said Ed. "First Edna dies, and then yer doin' the family tree. Any connection?"

"None," said Pete, but then he wondered, after all, if there was. Wasn't Martha's interest in finding a cousin due to the fact that there was now "no one else"?

"Myra's startin' to say there is," began Ed, "and nobody believed it; then all of a sudden everybody's believin' it. Just don't know if they're believin' it 'cause the same one lie got told so often it came back 'round from the other side lookin' like the truth, or if they started believin' it 'cause somethin' truthlike got into it, know what I mean?"

Pete did. He turned to ask Evan a question, but Evan got to him first.

"Chief bein' out to yer place didn't help any, Pete. And twice out to Martha's."

"I found her, for Pete's sake! And it's Martha's mother. The chief had a few questions. Did you know Lizzie Denault, Ev?"

"Knew of her, more like," said Evan. That was the trouble with Evan. With Ed or Bert, it was like a faucet without a shut-off valve. With Evan, it was like milking a cow when you didn't know how.

"You were friendly?"

Evan shrugged. The floor seemed to be interesting to Evan. "Friendly enough. Just didn't bother much with her."

From the other side, Bert Barker gave a loud snort. "Ya mean she didn't much bother with you, Ev!"

Pete looked again at Evan and wondered. He was a long-time bachelor, but Pete could see where a woman might bother with him: He had that so-called rugged profile of a person who worked outdoors a lot, offset by intelligence around the eyes. If Evan had wanted to bother with Lizzie, Pete wouldn't have been much surprised if Lizzie had bothered back. But had he?

"Wasn't my type," said Evan, not much daunted by Bert.

"She have any boyfriends you recall?" asked Pete, and Bert Barker snorted again.

"Who didn't she have?"

"Anyone I might know?"

"Whatcha wanna know for?" asked Ed. "This important to the family tree?"

Bert chimed in: "Some tree! They put all her ole boyfriends in, they'll get Sherwood Forest!"

"I need more information on Lizzie," continued Pete, "and it's a long story. I thought there might be someone who knew her I could talk to. Did anyone from the base ever come around the Denault—"

"Did anyone from the base come 'round!" hooted Bert. "The lawn looked like a Jeep shop!"

"Do you remember any names?" Pete was looking at Evan, but Evan was still looking at the floor, holding his empty Coke bottle between his knees.

"Lizzie didn't take names," said Bert, and Ed Healey chuckled and shook Evan along the bench closer to Pete.

"Nobody remembers a guy named Hal?"

"Hal," said Ed. "Was that the big guy with red hair?"

"Christamighty, Ed! That was Bernard somethin'. Some long thing. He didn't hang around Lizzie; that was after. Long after. Christ, Ed. Now Pete, whatcha think about Martha comin' back here all of a sudden like this?"

"Her mother died, Bert," said Pete, in what he felt was a neutral tone, but all three faces turned to look at him keenly, and at once he felt his face grow red.

"Yeah? So? Didn't seem to traipse back on-island when her pappy died, now did she?"

"Lizzie wasn't what they're sayin'," said Evan out of the side of his mouth from next to Pete. "But you ask Bob Wampeet about Lizzie."

Bob Wampeet was an Indian who ran the hotdog stand at the dock.

"What about—" Pete began, but now Ed Healey was picking up on Martha.

"Didn't like her mother much, Martha didn't," he said. "And I s'pose it's Martha hired ya 'bout this tree. Ya know somethin' yer not tellin'?"

Evan Spender stood up and moved toward the

steps. Pete tossed off the last of his Coke, intending to follow Evan to pursue the Bob Wampeet thing. Behind him, Ed and Bert continued on about Martha, but Pete didn't plan to stay long enough to listen.

"The Bean's gonna hafta be pretty careful," said Bert. "She's a tricky one. I wouldn't bet five cents he'll get anythin' on her, but I'll bet five Cokes she's mixed up in it wrong. Five Cokes."

"The Big Bean," said Ed, and this time *he* snorted. "Whatcha say, Pete? Five Cokes says Willy won't."

"Willy or won't he!" cackled Bert.

"Won't what?" asked Pete crossly, trying to pretend he hadn't heard. He had deposited his empty bottle in the crate beside the Coke machine under the hand-lettered sign that George Beston had tacked above it, reading "Leave the Bottle or I Raise the Price!" Pete moved down onto the first of the steps.

"Won't get anythin' on her. Won't figure it out a'tall. Whatcha say?"

"He's not as dumb as he looks," said Pete, wondering as he said it if he meant it, and why it was making him so worried, and why he hadn't jumped to the defense of Martha more. He moved down two more steps, but he didn't move down them far enough.

"Y'know Connie's been lookin' for ya," said Ed. "Ya hidin'?"

"No," said Pete, but even as he spoke he looked nervously down the street. He clumped down the remaining steps and moved across the dirt toward his truck.

"She hung out here yesterday awhile; we had

some laughs. She and Glen went bust, but I figure ya know that, huh?"

Pete put his hand on the door handle of his truck.

"I'll tell you who I sure never figured to go bust," Ed called after him. "I sure never figured you and her to go bust, I never did. She's lookin' for a place. Had some deal goin' that fell through . . ."

Pete got into the truck and slammed the door.

"Well anyway!" Ed hollered. "I see her again, I'll tell her ya say hi!"

Pete was halfway to Factotum before he remembered he'd been going to follow Evan's truck to ask him about Bob Wampeet. Oh well, he could just go straight to the dock and talk to Bob now, couldn't he? He pulled a U-turn and headed for the dock, but he hadn't quite turned into the parking lot by the Whiteaker when he saw the TR-6. He straightened out and kept going, paying no attention to which way he turned, seeing Connie's pale green eyes and flashing hair in every beach plum bush, thinking confused thoughts that seemed to keep mixing up Connie and Martha.

Somehow he was back on Main Street, and there was the town hall. What the heck, maybe Myra had gotten industrious—after all, she had had two whole days; it was either that or going back to Factotum to hang out with Rita and worry about the summer help. Maybe Myra was over this thing about Uncle Harmon by now.

Apparently she was. She handed Pete a manila folder full of photocopies of birth and death certificates, and she tried to tell him about each one of them, but Pete was getting good at these running farewells by now and was already in the truck before she had quite wound down. He sat in the truck and leafed through the documents and found them much as he had expected: Martha's father had died of a heart attack a year before, her grandparents had died when Martha was seventeen, within six months of each other. Lizzie had died in . . . He stopped and stared at Lizzie's death certificate. The cause of death was not drowning. She had died of respiratory failure secondary to an overdose of barbiturates and alcohol, just like Edna. Pete took another swing by the boathouse, but this time the VW was gone.

Chapter
11

Nashtoba had only one school that ran all the way
from kindergarten through the twelfth grade. Over
on the Hook things were regional, and every year
at town meeting another group of progressive new-
comers to the island brought up the subject of
Nashtoba joining in with the region, keeping
grades K through eight or so here and shipping the
older kids over the plank. It's not right, they said,
for some five-year-olds to be in the same building
with the punked-out twelfth graders. The region
would have better teachers, they said, thinking for
some reason that because teachers were from off-
island they were somehow more full of facts. Pete
didn't have any kids and he didn't know anything
about schools, except what he remembered from
being in them. It had had its good points, the little
school on Nashtoba: Everyone knew everyone and
cared about what everyone did. It had had its bad
points, also: Everyone knew everyone and cared
about what everyone did. At this present point in
his life, Pete interfaced with his old school only

once a week, on Thursdays in the gym, for a pick-up game of basketball, and he was unable to walk up the brick steps and down the linoleum halls without hearing echoes of all those good/bad old days: Peter! This is no way to hand in a piece of homework. I heard about your grandmother and I guess this wasn't your best week, so I'm accepting this, this once and this once only. Peter! This is no way to hand in a piece of homework. I saw your bike at Lucy's till past ten last night, so don't give me this nonsense about how hard you tried! I know how hard you tried, young man, and it wasn't anything to do with your math homework! F!

They played shirts and skins in the gym, eight or ten of the over-the-hill crowd, every Thursday, all year round. That Thursday they were sitting on the bottom bleacher, sorting themselves into two teams. The shirts were just letting out secret sighs of relief that they were going to be shirts, and the skins were taking a few preparatory deep breaths to get ready for the hardest part of the sport—holding in the beer gut for two hours without letting anyone know you were doing it. Pete's head was somewhere inside his T-shirt when he felt the change in the air as Chief Will McOwat walked into the gym.

"Chief!" he said in surprise, as his head squirmed out.

"Willy, please," said the chief. "Need a man?"

Pete looked at the bench. Six men sat on it. Four on three wasn't the best pick-up game in the world, and still nobody spoke. "Yeah," said Pete, "skins need a man." Pete's team always seemed to be the one short a man, and Pete was astute enough to know that it was in good part because it *was* Pete's team that it was always left short: Pete had a strenuous job that left him with a good set of muscles, and he had a limited fascination for beer and had to waste no wind holding in his gut; consequently, not only was he good for at least one fast break a night, he would often average two or more three-pointers. The four shirts—Jerry Beggs, Leon Price, Dave Snow, and Wally Melville—glared at him, but as the large police chief struggled out of his shirt and displayed a gut there was no point in trying to suppress, their faces brightened. The Big Bean, Pete knew in a flash, was going to get creamed.

He did. He got elbows in the face, knees in his side, one slam that sent him into the water fountain and another that crashed him down to the floor. After Leon Price tried to put his elbow into Willy's nose by going straight down through the bone, Pete started to get mad. He'd always had this embarrassing defense-of-underdog mode that he slipped into almost automatically. He decked Leon with a right shoulder to the chest and at the end of the game waited beside Willy at the side of the court, slimy with sweat, as The Bean leaned over and gulped air as the rest of the guys filed past and gave him now-friendly slaps on the back. When he could hear himself over the sound of the chief's wheezing, he said, "Beer?" secure in making the offer, since he knew the chief would say no.

"Sure," said Willy, and he straightened up and led the way out.

Pete wasn't sure how it happened—how all the rest of them were at their usual seats at the bar, and Pete was stuck with Willy at a table in the corner—but somehow Pete began to get the idea that the whole thing wasn't exactly an accident. Willy paid for the first round, then took out a mangled cigarette and began to twirl it around in his fingers.

"I quit," he explained, and then, maybe recalling his recent performance on the courts, he added, "recently." He drained off half of his beer and gave a deep, happy sigh. "So!" he said, and he grinned at Pete. "Next week Leon gets his head taken off."

Next week? "Old Leon usually lays into me pretty bad," said Pete, by way of making Willy feel less picked upon. He noticed Willy's beer was now empty, and he ordered another round, tossing his own off as he did so. It tasted good. Too good.

"Married?" asked Willy.

Pete shook his head, fighting off an urge to explain further.

"Me either. Funny thing." The chief didn't elaborate, but Pete had been thinking that same thing, of late. It was getting so that the happily married Bill Freeds were few and far between these days, although Bill's marriage was not one that Pete would ever have settled for himself or have been particularly tempted to call happy.

The chief took a long pull at his beer and sighed again. Pete took a cautious sip of his own. He didn't suppose a police chief would keep ordering a person beers and then arrest him as he drove off, would he?

"This place," Willy began, and he shook his head. He looked out Lupo's doorway in the direction of the water. "You'd never think a person could get up enough steam to kill someone here, now would you?''

"Oh, I dunno," said Pete. The island seemed to Pete to be full of feisty, crusty types who could get riled pretty fast and stay mad pretty long. He was thinking of Sarah, and Hardy, and . . . They think I did it, Martha had said. Pete drained his second glass, and Willy ordered two more.

"How well do you know Martha Hitchcock, Pete?"

Careful, thought Pete. We are now officially on The Subject. "Not at all," he answered. "She was mostly away. She was at school off-island, and summer camp a lot, and then she was . . . away." Cripes! He was already babbling.

Willy McOwat didn't seem to hear. He was back on the subject of Nashtoba. "I like it here. At least I *could* like it here. If I last long enough I'd like to buy a house, the small cape on Shore Road, by all the scrub pines—you know the one I mean?"

The whole island was covered with scrub pines, and Shore Road was just about exactly twice as long as the island itself, but Pete as a matter of fact did know just the one he meant. "Buy it now," he said. "I hear Nate Cox is getting into it." Nate Cox was the new realtor. Once Nate Cox got into things, the price usually upped another third.

Willy sighed. "Yeah. Story of my life. If I last through this . . ."

Pete did not need to ask, through what. From somewhere two more beers appeared, and Pete was only a third into his previous one. That was what happened at Lupo's: They started lining them up on you, and you kept on drinking them just to be polite.

The chief was mumbling something about politics and results. All of a sudden he looked Pete straight in the eye, the crow's feet at the corners of his own eyes hardening. "So what's this genealogy I've been hearing about, Pete?"

Pete swallowed some beer. "Genealogy?" The chief didn't bother to ask him again or clarify his question. After mulling things over in a muddled sort of way, Pete explained everything about the job he had been hired to do for Martha.

The chief nodded as he listened, but he never took his eyes off of Pete's, and when Pete got through with the description of the actual job, the chief asked, "So what's the general plan? How would you go about something like that?"

It was all beginning to sound official. Pete thought a minute and then tried to sound, if not official, at least organized. He mentally visualized his yellow pad and outlined for the chief the steps he had already taken and then the ones he planned to take in the near future. By the time he'd finished he had reduced the two beers in front of him back to one, and the next one was already arriving. He wasn't going to last much longer, he realized, and if this was going to get official he had a few questions of his own he wanted to work in. He wanted, above all, to find out just how concerned Willy was about that Seconal bottle that Martha brought to Hardy's, how much play he was planning to give to all the garbage about the will. He wanted to ask Willy if he truly thought Martha did it, but how could he bring any of that up without giving it more play just by talking about it? "Would it be possible to see a copy of the old police report on

Lizzie Denault's death?'' he asked instead, and he explained to the chief why he wanted to see it.

Willy made a noncommittal sound into his beer.

Pete tried something else. "This Seconal that Edna Hitchcock took the day she died: Is it possible it could have been in the liquor bottle? If it was in the bottle itself, someone could have put it there long ago."

The chief gazed lazily at Pete. "No trace in the bottle," he said. "It was all in the glass."

"Oh," said Pete. "Well, what about this hot water? You know, they say if you drink in your jacuzzi you can pass right out. You don't suppose someone filled the tub with hot water to make it appear to have been an accident like that?"

"I agree with you that the hot water is the key," said Willy; then he straightened up and waved at the waitress. Pete attempted to beat him to it, but Willy waved him away and bought him yet another beer. He was approaching serious trouble.

"Would you say Martha Hitchcock was pretty popular around here?" Willy asked, and Pete could see how the whole thing was shaping up. You buy the beer, you ask the questions—simple as that.

"No," said Pete, thinking of the talk on Beston's porch.

"Why not?"

"She left," said Pete. "Nobody could keep track of her. Around here people like to be able to keep track of what you do. Around here people figure if you don't stick around there's either something wrong with you yourself or with what you're doing." And why—now, again—was he thinking of Connie?

"Or if you're from someplace else to start with," said Willy, and Pete had no trouble figuring what he was thinking about.

"Yes." He cleared his throat. "And someone like Martha isn't the type to go around letting her own feelings be known. I don't think she lets on even to herself sometimes. And when these people can't tell what you're thinking, they assume you're thinking the worst, and they assume it's about them."

"Well, she's sure as hell more popular than me," said Willy, and he slammed a few dollars onto the bar and stood up. "When you get around to those neighbors out at the Point, I'd be interested in a few things. Did anyone see anything strange, any strange cars, on June 15? Who were Edna's usual visitors?" Willy looked behind him at the row of basketball players at the bar. He squinted into the bar light as if considering something of grave weight, then turned back to Pete. He pulled a twenty out of his wallet. "A round for the bar." He slapped Pete on the shoulder and left Lupo's, apparently untouched by numerous beers. Pete stood up to join the gang at the bar, and, having to take a half step sideways to keep on his feet, he changed his mind and turned for the door instead. It's all to do with body fat, he told himself: The more beer you drink the fatter you get, and the fatter you get, the more beer you can drink. He was mulling over the idea of writing something up on his fat-beer-fat theory for a medical journal, and wishing that Nashtoba would break down and paint a few lines on its roads, when creepy little feelers of a thought started worming into the cracks of his brain. Why did Willy McOwat come to basketball in the first place? He couldn't shoot, he had no wind, and he didn't even bang around under the boards like the rest of them. The feelers couldn't quite take root, but Pete drove home left with a conviction that he should leave Bob Wampeet for now, call the lawyer and Rematch and the adoption agencies at some later date, and start in on the neighbors at the Point; strange cars and strange visitors. Anyone other than Martha.

Chapter
12

Pete was in and out of Sarah's in fifteen minutes.
They were volatile around each other; that was the
only word for it. Why? Because she kept bringing
up Connie and making him mad. And he kept bringing up the Hitchcocks and making her upset. Of
course, it would make her upset: Someone she
knew was now dead, and it was probable that whoever did it was also known to her, and he did try
to keep them off the subject, but he just couldn't
seem to keep his mind off it. And as for Connie,
Sarah would get over all that once she realized
Connie meant nothing to him any more, and that
he meant nothing to her. After all, how long could
Connie possibly stay? Any day now she'd jump
back into that midlife crisis car of hers and blow
town. For a flash of a moment, Pete saw Connie
back in the house on the marsh, her feet up on the
end of the couch, eating popcorn and reading, and
he felt a stab of pain. It had seemed so great for
a while, and then just like that she was gone; there
should have been something between "great" and

"gone." True, Pete knew she had wanted to move—either move Factotum or move themselves; Pete had known that, must have known that. He had hoped she would get over it, get used to it; he had been unable to explain why he needed to stay, why he needed to keep the workings of Factotum near at hand. He was not a person who adjusted well to change, but he was learning about it now, and fast. He had once been unable to imagine life without Connie. . . . He shook his head and drove steadily on toward the Point. So that's how you adjusted to change—it came, you adjusted—and he was living without Connie fine. Just fine. It had been a lonely year, but he could feel that that was past him now and things were changing and he had adjusted and . . .

He was suddenly thinking of Martha. He looked down the list she had given him and at the first name on it: Muriel Hatch. "Friend of my mother's," Martha had written beside it.

They think I did it, she had said.

Sam and Brenda Hayes were next on the list. "Next door, south" was all she had written. And Henry Baker's house was beyond the Hayes house. "Has known family for years," Martha had written next to Henry. The only name Pete was really acquainted with was Henry's, but he decided to start with Muriel Hatch, partly because he didn't have to drive by The Spookhouse to get there.

They think I did it.

But why? Or, should he be asking, why not?

He pulled into the driveway of a big, three-story, glaringly white garrison with plastic lawn furniture with chartreuse cushions grouped in a stilted semicircle off to one side, and stiff balls and spikes of foundation plants across the front, under windows with diaphanous curtains. Pete had hated the house ever since it had been built six years before, but he had never really noticed until now how all its accouterments were so well suited. One of the curtains pulled back and dropped down.

Muriel Hatch herself went with the accouterments well. She should have had several scrawny kids hanging off her housecoat and an unemployed husband who sat around in his T-shirt, watching TV.

"Are you another cop?" she asked. She had narrow, pinky-blue eyes and gray roots showing at the base of reddish-yellow hair. This was a friend of Edna's?

"No, I'm not," began Pete. "I'm not here in relation to any crime that may recently have—"

"*May* recently have! That poor woman. And to think of that girl . . . I can only say I'm glad she's not alive to see it."

"I'm not with the police, Mrs. Hatch. Mrs. Hatch?"

The woman gave a half nod; maybe yes, maybe no.

"My name is Peter Bartholomew—Factotum. Have you heard of us?"

She shook her head, frowning, her posture subtly transforming into what must have been her standard defense-against-the-Fuller-brush-man pose.

"I'm working for the Hitchcock family. I'm specifically trying to gather information about Edna Hitchcock's sister, Elizabeth Denault. . . ."

"Working for the family. Must be the girl, then. Trying to crawl out from under the rap?"

Pete cleared his throat. "If you would rather not speak with me . . ."

Paradoxically, that seemed to do the trick.

"You want to sit down or something?"

Pete wasn't sure that he did, but he followed her into the living room anyway. There were modular units of white furniture and a glass-enclosed fireplace, all detracting from the large picture window that faced the sea. He didn't like it, and he thought, again, of Edna's meticulous person and what he had glimpsed of her house—all ginger jars and sea chests and expensive brocade. Muriel Hatch and Edna? Friends? Pete perched on the corner of one of the fluffy white squares that reminded him of marshmallows and immediately fell in and back. He struggled back up to the edge and smiled at Muriel Hatch. She smiled back. She waved a finger, upon which a large, uninteresting diamond was perched.

"You sure you're not a cop?"

"Factotum," said Pete, again. "Persons employed to do all kinds of work. Martha Hitchcock hired me to find out what I could about her aunt, Edna's sister, Elizabeth. Martha never knew her, but she recently decided—"

"I bet she recently decided! Bump off the old lady and then send the spies around to see how much we know! She's clever, I'll give her that."

Pete shifted his rear end in the marshmallow and pulled at his chinos and remembered Hardy Rogers. Martha had brought in a bottle of Seconal in May and brought it back out, and Pete still hadn't found out where it was. In that jar in the morgue? No.

Muriel Hatch had seated herself on the raised

flagstone hearth and was pulling her housedress down hard over swollen knees. "I've been here six years and I never heard Edna mention any sister Elizabeth. You'd better look sharp—that girl's taking you for a ride."

"Edna's sister is dead. She died over thirty years ago. Edna never mentioned it to you? They called her Lizzie."

Muriel Hatch didn't seem to want to say, no, she had never heard Edna mention this person; but at the same time she seemed unable to say, yes, she had. She changed the subject, sort of. "Around this place you'd be lucky to hear the time. Some neighborhood. The only friendly one was Edna." Muriel Hatch's face shriveled up into what must have been her thinking mode. "Factotum," she said. "Yes, I have heard of you. I called you people to get some lawn furniture painted and they told me I had to wait three weeks. Three weeks!"

Pete stood up. A thousand dollars was only, after all, a thousand dollars. "Thank you, Mrs. Hatch. I'm sorry to have bothered you."

Mrs. Hatch didn't get up. "Edna came here lots. She and I used to have a little drink in the afternoons and talk about our kids. Kids! Do everything for them and all they want is more. And what do they do back for you? Nothing!" She switched from kids to men. "Frank Hitchcock wasn't a bit like Edna. He never said two words to us. I think he was mad when we built this place, as if he should care! It's not like you can see anyone from one house to another—they're miles apart! But he was always moping around the beach and glaring up at us, ignoring everyone but himself—typical man. Never around, and then won't believe it when the kids turn out wrong. Or worse, pretends it's all your fault!"

Pete had stopped moving toward the door. Almost against his will, he had turned around and resumed his spot on the marshmallow. "Do you mean Mr. Hitchcock got along with Martha no better than his wife did?"

Muriel Hatch could see that she was recapturing her audience. "He must have gotten along some better, taking all Edna told me about the money and all, him leaving all his money to Martha. Of course, the house was Edna's, but that was another funny thing. She wanted to sell out and he wouldn't let her. Her own house and he wouldn't let her! I always figured he must have held something over her, but she never told me what. Didn't blame her for hating it, that ramshackle old thing. She wanted a house like mine." Muriel Hatch looked around, and, seeming to realize she wasn't showing it off to its best advantage, she got up and sat down gingerly in one of the white puff chairs. "Of course, I have to hand it to Edna: She did up the inside pretty nice. You've seen it?"

Pete nodded. He refrained from saying that it was the outside that he liked. He wanted to go, but he still had a few questions left to ask . . . for Willy. "Besides yourself, did Mrs. Hitchcock have other close friends?"

Muriel Hatch gave a short bark. "Here? Friends?"

"I suppose," Pete continued, feeling foolish, "you don't ever see many cars way out here. I suppose if you see one you don't recognize, it's an occasion of sorts."

106

Muriel Hatch humphed. "When I first came here I'd go right out if I saw a car, thinking it was someone being friendly. Not a chance! Oh, they maybe stopped once or twice, when I first came; now I don't even look out the window any more. I couldn't tell you the first thing about cars by here. Of course, I can tell you when Brenda Hayes has been shopping—those three kids strapped in the back seat and shopping bags to the roof in the back of that wagon. And of course, Henry Baker's old Nova sounds like a whale coming up for air! Honestly, he shouldn't be driving at all. I sometimes wonder what this police department does all day if it can't keep a menace like Henry off the road. Do you know Edna told me he's had that old blue car for fifteen years? Fifteen years! And he can't see his hand in front of his face, I bet you any money he can't. Now, when Frank was alive—Frank, that's Edna's husband—he had this white Skylark and Edna had the white Dodge, and you couldn't tell one from the other except by the way they drove. Talk about cautious! That Frank, I tell you, it must have taken him two days to get to the post office." Here Muriel Hatch leaned forward. "Of course, I'm not one to go blabbing everything odd I see," she said. "And when the police asked me, I kept my trap tight shut. When you're not sure you don't speak—that's what I always say."

Pete swallowed. "Something odd?"

"I just happened to be going by the Sunday night before Edna died, and I did see a strange car. One of those English sports cars with a convertible top. Dark green. And the top was black. Marked up, not new, but I knew it was one of those English ones because I'd seen one like it with one of those English flags.''

Pete stopped breathing, then started up again, too fast. "You saw this car where?"

"In Edna's drive. The night before she was killed. Wasn't any car I knew."

"And you say you didn't mention this to the police?"

Muriel Hatch lifted her chin. "And why should I? What has this place ever told me? I walk in the store and they all stop talking. Bunch of loonies, I tell you! All inbred, you know. . . ." Something seemed to make her think better of continuing in that vein. Pete soon found out what it was.

"You're not from here originally, are you? I mean . . . originally?"

Pete stood up, and this time he moved steadily toward the door. "Sure am," he said. "I'm one of the loonies. But only on my father's side."

Chapter
13

Rita was getting frantic over the ringing phone. It never used to bother her—she could answer it while doing something else and be half thinking of a third thing—but now she was getting muddled and she couldn't seem to keep her mind on two things at once, let alone three. Factotum was busy, and they kept Bill hopping with last-minute presummer things: awnings to be hung, shutters to be painted, moorings to be buried—this year more than ever, now that Pete was off chasing fictitious cousins all over the place. The whole thing was odd, to say the least, and Rita spent a few minutes each day mulling over their various relationships with Martha and Edna Hitchcock and how Pete had come to be so central to it all. And the other odd thing was Bill. For months he hadn't broken a thing, and now he was tripping all over himself again and disappearing at odd hours. . . . And then there was the small matter of the third thing that was on her mind, the third thing responsible for the slipping of her own gears and the shelving of the number-one and -two troubles: John Clark.

It was funny. Rita liked herself all right; she knew what she was and what she wasn't, or at least she had thought she did. She knew she was okay to look at, she took pains with herself, but she knew there was something about her that attracted only a certain type of man. She was the motherly sort, and Rita was sick to death of mothering. She was sick to death of everyone else having all the fun: Bill off being mysterious, taking courses; Pete—let's face it, Pete was getting hot and bothered over Martha. And where did that leave Rita? Then, just when it appeared that once again everyone but Rita was going to be off doing interesting things, *poom!* John Clark backs into Martha. Good-looking John Clark. Polished. Poised. And interested. In her. For once in her life, Rita had been in the right place at the right time and had said the right thing: yes! And there she was, having fun!

"Yes," said Rita into the phone when she should very possibly have said "no"; and "yes," she said again, when John called to ask her to lunch. She piled the employment applications that had already been completed on Pete's desk with a big note that said "Read!" and she left for lunch with John.

Pete drove by The Spookhouse without even noticing it and pulled up in front of the Hayes house on the opposite side. Which way would Connie have gone, he wondered, when she left Edna's? Left, past Muriel's, or right, past the Hayes house? Assuming of course that the English sports car with the green paint and black top was Connie's, which could be assuming a lot. Couldn't it?

Brenda Hayes opened the door to him and smiled. She had red hair and white, white skin that turned a shocking red all its own the minute he mentioned the Hitchcock name. Was she blushing? Pete explained his business and soon discovered that the red was not from embarrassment but from fury.

"Hitchcock!" she spat. But the door was held open, so Pete walked in. Fools rush; he moved slowly, and in consequence he was lined up with his ear directly across from her lips when she let go full force. "Hitchcock!"

Pete jumped. Brenda Hayes pointed a finger in his face. By now the flush from her face had spread all the way downward into the V of her sweater and disappeared from view. The sweater was tight, and Pete spent some seconds examining it.

"Don't you say that name to me again!" hollered Brenda. "Don't you set foot in this house with that name in your mouth! Come in!"

Pete considered the contradictory directions and decided to go with the last one. He followed Brenda Hayes into a room on the south side of the house that was full of plants and glass and white metal furniture. If the sun ever came to Nashtoba again, the room would be flooded with it. Brenda Hayes flopped down onto a metal chair, and Pete took the one across from her. He was almost afraid to look up.

"You said you were here about Martha," said Brenda. She had quieted down on her walk through the house, it seemed. "I don't have anything against Martha. You just keep the name of her mother out of my house." She leaned toward him. The pink had been receding, but as she spoke again it began to ebb downward. "And I don't give a damn that she's dead! It doesn't fix anything. It doesn't fix my daughter's face."

"Your daughter's . . ."

Brenda whipped around and banged on the glass as three blond heads went tearing by. "Heidi! Come in here!"

It was the largest of the three small girls who came in through the sun-room door and up to her mother with caution. Brenda Hayes pulled her by the elbow until she was standing close, faced her to Pete, and swept back the long bangs of fine hair. A mauve scar ran from Heidi's right temple down the side of her face and curved into her cheek. Brenda pulled the little girl into her sweater and gave her a fierce hug and four kisses. "Go," she said. Heidi went. The two smaller children who had waited outside the door, peeking in, scooped Heidi up and then shot off, out of view. Were they all used to this displaying of Heidi's wound? Pete wondered. And which was worse, after all: the wound or this drama surrounding it?

Brenda Hayes was wiping tears from her eyes, and Pete was beginning to think a thousand dollars was not nearly enough. He leaned forward and touched Brenda's knee in what stopped just short of being a reassuring pat.

"Edna Hitchcock did that," said Brenda. "Last October. Came hellbent around the turn, stinking full of booze, and careened right up onto the lawn. Careened right off it again, of course, but not till she'd knocked Heidi out into the road. Screwed

112

some cop or something so he'd lie about it all. Said she was 'exhibiting no evidence of intoxication' and so no Breathalyzer test was given. Said she was in the road and my Heidi ran out. They tried to make it my fault, as if I wasn't watching my daughter; that was what they were trying to say. Why wasn't I watching my daughter? Why did I let her play in the road on that bad turn?'' Brenda Hayes's voice was now half dead, the red flame of her fury long gone. She looked up at Pete and tried to smile. "So, what was it you wanted to know?"

"I'm sorry," said Pete. "About your daughter. I hardly noticed it until . . ."

She smiled at him more successfully this time. "Everyone tells me that. And she's supposed to have more surgery next fall. But to me it's like someone took a red-hot poker and . . ." Tears again. "It wouldn't be so bad if she were a boy."

Pete felt the hair on the back of his neck start to stand up. Why not! he wanted to say. He had hoped the days of Miss Teenage America were coming to a close. He flipped open a notepad, cleared his throat, and asked his questions about Elizabeth Denault, determining that Brenda had heard of her, had heard of the drowning, and then more recently (already!) that she hadn't really drowned at all. Beyond that she was no help, but when Pete switched from the past to the present, and to cars on the road, Brenda came to life and sat up. "Ever since that accident I've been antsy about cars on that road. I hear one and I tear to the window to see where the kids are, even if they're right inside under my feet! I've told them they are absolutely not allowed in the front of the house—not ever—but it's so windy out back by the water that they creep around to the sides and it makes me nervous. . . . Anyway, I think I've seen every car down this road since last October, and that's not many cars, I can tell you. If you come from town you go the other way, see? And that Edna had no friends, I can tell you that; just that disgusting Muriel Hatch from the other side. Anyway, the day Edna died, it seemed to me like there was traffic up and down that road all day. In the morning I remember a dark green car I'd never seen before, and later in the afternoon a sort of burgundy-colored one, and just before dark there was this old beat-up truck.'' She stopped, and her eyes widened and a dusting of fuchsia broke out on her cheeks and chest. ''Yours, I think?''

Pete grinned. ''I claim the beat-up old truck.'' He looked down at his notebook, which was empty. ''You say you saw a dark green car? Could you describe it?''

She shrugged her shoulders, looked into Pete's eyes, and gave a sheepish grin. ''I'm a car moron,'' she said. ''It was dark green. It wasn't really very big, I don't think. . . .'' She shrugged. ''That's it.''

''Convertible? Hardtop?''

She frowned, thinking. ''Gee. It had a top, I know that, so maybe that means it was hard? I really didn't notice.''

''What color was the top?''

Brenda sighed. ''The whole car was dark. I'm not sure if the top was just the same green as the car or . . .'' Her face brightened up. ''The burgundy one was one of those hatchback types. Or maybe it was one of those tiny little station wagons, you know? Neither car was anything anyone on the Point drives, I can tell you that."

"And this was Monday, the fifteenth, you say? The green car? Monday, not Sunday night?"

Brenda Hayes tipped her head sideways and gave him her first really good look. "You know, if I didn't know them all and if I hadn't already talked to them all three times over, I'd bet you were with the police."

Pete coughed. "I'm not. I know it may seem odd, these questions, but I . . ." But what? He was never good at lying. And this woman had been straightforward with him. "I'm worried about someone," he finished, and amazingly, this seemed to satisfy her.

"So don't even try to explain. It's none of my business. I'm kind of glad to be talking to you, to tell you the truth. I probably should have said something about the cars to the police, but I didn't want to, not knowing whose they were or really if I were remembering right. But I can't stop thinking about it, just the same, and I'm glad I've told *someone,* at least."

Pete stared at her. So she hadn't told Willy about the cars, either. This place.

Brenda leaned back in her chair, pulled one foot up under her, and looked at the plant over her head. "Sunday. Nope. Nobody but the doctor. I seem to recall some lights going by later, but the kids were all in bed so I didn't bother to look." She sat back and smiled at him.

"The doctor was there?"

"Hardy. Sunday afternoon. I remember that; he drives a Volvo station wagon, and that I know

115

because Sam, my husband, had one just like it.
Hardy stops in on Edna now and then."

He does, does he?

"But the maroon station wagon on Sunday was
not the same car that you call burgundy, which
was here Monday?"

Brenda looked at him and raised one eyebrow.
"I think I'd have noticed right off if that Monday
car was Hardy's. That's not who you're worried
about, is it? Hardy?"

"No," said Pete. Who *was* he worried about? It
had started out to be Martha, but somewhere along
the line something had changed. Martha's and Connie's faces were playing tricks on him, switching
back and forth, similar cloudy hair and sea-green
eyes dancing between a wide-open expression of
disdain on the one hand and that shuttered look of
hurt on the other. And then even the expressions
seemed to switch on him, and the woman in the
green Triumph hopped out over the top of the door
and jumped into the yellow VW and . . . He shook
his head.

"Thank you," he said to Brenda Hayes.
"You've been a big help."

But had she?

Martha had stopped answering her phone, and
now she was learning how dangerous that practice
could be. Once you stopped answering your
phone, they began arriving at your door, one by
one, two by two. . . . On Friday it was Bill. He
began with reason, moved on to tears, and finished
off with threats.

On Saturday it was, of all people, Rita Peck and
John Clark. She was startled when she entered the

kitchen and saw them through the glass, a couple in weekend clothes that only people like Rita Peck and John Clark would wear: Rita in white pants and a turquoise sweater that went great with her black hair; John in tan twill, boat shoes, and an off-white sweater without a shirt.

"I hadn't seen you," explained Rita. "We did try calling. John was concerned that you were all right."

"Sometimes after a bump like that you can get quite a sore neck," said John Clark. "When Rita was unable to reach you . . ."

"I don't answer my phone much," said Martha.

Rita smiled uneasily. John Clark's smile came off with more ease.

Martha didn't ask them in, so after a second's pause, Rita chattered on.

"Well, John feels just awfully about it, anyway," she said, "and he wants to make it up to us. You. He wants to take us out to dinner. At the Whiteaker. On the Fourth. The tables on the porch look right out over the fireworks on the Hook."

"How does that sound?" asked John Clark.

Rotten, thought Martha. But she had long before learned how fastest to get rid of people—lie.

"If I'm free that would be nice," she answered them, and she almost laughed out loud at her own choice of words. The significance was not lost on her guests: They exchanged a glance that told her they had been talking about her a bit, but she didn't even care.

"You could bring a date, couldn't she, John? I know we were thinking of asking Pete. . . ."

"I won't be planning on bringing a date," said Martha. Both John Clark and Rita were watching her closely. They both now smiled. What was this, a fix-up? Martha groaned. But what did it matter, since she had no intention of going anyway.

And on Sunday it was Peter Bartholomew himself. She asked *him* in and offered him a drink, and he selected a beer. Martha made a daiquiri for herself. They sat in the living room, Martha on the cot, Pete in the rocking chair, his legs stretched out straight in front of him, the old-fashioned low-cut basketball sneakers with rubber toes crossed. Martha looked at the sneakers and listened to his voice as he began to tell her about Lizzie, and something that was wound tightly clockwise in her began a slow, counterclockwise turn. Lizzie had had a baby. She had not really drowned. Pete's voice went smoothly on. Then all of a sudden they weren't talking about Lizzie any more; they were talking about the bottle of pills, and the rocking chair was rocking and Martha's inner spring had twisted back up. The rocking stopped. The sneakers moved. He leaned forward and touched her wrist.

"I'm not looking for you to explain anything to *me*," he said. She looked up at his face and quickly back down at the sneaks. It was true; he wasn't looking for that. He was looking at her as if whatever she had done with the pills was all right with him, as if nothing could ever be her fault. Why?

"But Hardy feels—and I have to agree—that you had better tell the chief a little something more. There are other places they should be looking, and they won't be doing that if they feel they are safe in concentrating on you. That makes sense, doesn't it?"

Martha didn't answer.

"Doesn't it?" he said again, and Martha looked up fast and then down again at her friends, the sneakers. Okay, so high-tops were back in, but who in the world still walked around in those short basketball sneakers with rubber toes? She began to speak to the sneakers.

"The house at the Point belonged to my mother," she said. "My father knew that if he died first my mother would sell it; she never really liked it here. He was able to persuade her to stay while he was alive, and he made arrangements so I wouldn't have to lose it if he died. He left me a lot of money so I could buy the house from my mother. He left my mother some money, but not a lot, thinking that after I gave her the money for the house it would even out." The sneakers didn't move or speak.

"My mother was angry about the money, of course. That was part of it. But there were other things. He left instructions that he did not want a funeral. None at all. She couldn't stand that. What would people think? What would happen to all the attention she was supposed to get? So she gave him a funeral and I didn't come to it and that did it. You can imagine what people were saying about that." She looked up again briefly. And what had *you* thought about it? she wondered. "So my mother decided to get even. She refused to sell me the house. She decided to stay on in it, a house she hated on an island she loathed, just so I could never have it. She held that house over my head every time she wanted me to do something, change something, be somebody I . . ." Martha stopped. She noticed her drink was empty and that Peter

Bartholomew seemed to be fascinated by the bottom of his bottle of beer. She got up and got them two more. I'm drinking too much, she thought. Talking too much. Why? "The night before she died, she called me up at my apartment in Boston and told me she was moving to Florida and renting out the house. She threw in that she was going to cut me out of her will; she wasn't going to leave the house to me." Martha gave a dry laugh that didn't sound like herself. "Who was she going to leave it to, the fish?" She looked down again, at the sneakers. "So the police chief knows about me and my mother. He knows about the will, that my mother was planning to change it. The police love stuff like that—real old-fashioned motives like wills and hatred." Martha looked up in time to see Pete wince. "So I don't remember what I did with the pills. Do you really think if I did, it would make any difference?"

After a few seconds of silence, Peter Bartholomew cleared his throat. "Your father must have known you loved that house very much. He must have loved *you* very much."

"I don't love that house any more," said Martha, and then Peter Bartholomew said a surprising thing.

"Me either," he said.

Late Monday, after Rita had left the office once again with John Clark and Pete was feeling peculiarly out of sorts, the chief knocked at his door.

"Here's that report you wanted," said the chief, thrusting a manila envelope into his hands.

"Wow!" said Pete. "Thanks!"—aware that he was sounding like a Hardy boy. He flipped open the envelope, and a large hand reached out and took it back.

"Later, if you don't mind," he said. "If you've got a minute, that is."

Pete looked at him closely. Since their game of basketball, Pete had learned that there were a few specifics in addition to the general unpopularity of The Big Bean that had set that game off into abusiveness: Willy had actually hauled in Dave Snow for OUI and ticketed Leon for doing forty on Main. Was The Bean here to be friends, or was he here mainly to . . .

"Been talking to the neighbors?" asked Willy, and that was sufficient explanation for Pete.

Pete nodded. This was okay. This was something that Pete had been anxious to talk to the chief about himself. He opened the door wider and offered up a beer, determined that this time he was providing the beer and this time he was going to ask the questions. As seemed to be the method with everyone who stopped around, they bypassed the lumpy rattan furniture in the living room/office area and went down the hall to the kitchen, and the beer, and the kitchen table and chairs.

"I have talked to a few of the neighbors," began Pete, sipping sedately at his beer, "and I can't help thinking there are quite a few areas of interest, and I'm a bit surprised that you seem to be ignoring them."

Willy stiffened and pulled at his ear, folding the top half down over the bottom. Was he tuning Pete out? "What do you think should be occupying my time then, huh? I take it you've got a theory." There was a touch of sarcasm weighing down the word *theory*.

Pete took another drink of beer and tried to blot out the image of an English sports car that suddenly came to mind. He cast around for other straws and found one. "There's what happened to Heidi, for example."

The chief frowned. "And who the hell is Heidi?"

Already Pete was feeling sorry he had said it. "Nothing, really. There was an accident in October, and Brenda was upset about the Breathalyzing, that's all." He tossed off the rest of his beer and looked down, expecting another one to have materialized the same way they did in Lupo's. It had not.

"What accident?" Willy's eyes were slits.

"Nothing," said Pete. "Really. Edna hit Brenda Hayes's little girl and . . ."

The chief pushed back his chair and strode out of the kitchen, leaving Pete awash in guilt at his own kitchen table.

And what would he have said to Willy if he had given Willy the chance to ask him about the cars?

Chapter
14

Connie picked another pink thread off her red sweater and frowned at Sarah. What is wrong with this picture? she asked herself. Sarah was playing poor-poor-pitiful-me, a role she did not play too often.

"First the energy surcharge and then the real-estate taxes," she was saying.

Connie waited. It didn't take long.

"So I've decided to take in a boarder. Summer's coming; I'm sure I could find someone who would like a room cheap."

"Good idea," said Connie.

Sarah's eyes narrowed behind her lenses. "What's the Whiteaker charging these days?"

"I'm working on a rental," Connie said quickly. "I won't be there long."

"Well thank God," said Sarah, in a tone more aptly suited to the phrase "go to hell," and all of a sudden Connie caved in.

What if she meant it, this manipulating old woman? What if things really were tight? And Connie noticed there were dustballs under the couch and all these goddamned threads all over the furniture. And every time Sarah sat down, the chair looked like it wobbled. *Was* it time that Sarah not live alone?

"Of course," said Connie, "if you wanted to beat their offer . . ."

The bright eyes behind the glasses grew brighter. "Thirty a week. And we split the food."

"Deal," said Connie. "And I can do the shopping."

Sarah waved a hand the color and texture of worn pine. "Pete does that," she said, and Connie looked hard at her. Was that the game? If it was, the joke was going to be on Sarah. Once Pete found out Connie was staying here, she doubted very much if he'd be coming around, doing shopping or anything else, and it would only be fair to warn her.

"Pete's pretty busy with that Hitchcock thing, I hear," she said. "And since I'm not busy with anything, yet . . ." She had planned to take the summer off, to look around, to see how she liked it, being back; then maybe she could line up a teaching job for the fall, if she really felt like staying. . . .

Was it her imagination, or was Sarah's hand on her cane beginning to shake? It's a good thing, thought Connie, that I'm going to be around. I think.

It was the first hot day. It was typical Nashtoba, leaving you in one overnight span to adjust to the fact that not only did you now not need your long-sleeved sweaters, but even all the doors and windows opened wide to the ocean breeze couldn't get the air to move, the heat to rise up from where it was choking you in the chest. Pete had spent the majority of the day painting the Rinaldis' boat and had just showered and changed and was sitting on his porch, trying to pretend he didn't really want a beer, wondering if up on Martha's dune the breeze would be any better. Then he remembered that he did have Willy's report on Aunt Lizzie to show her, and suddenly he felt a little perkier. He grabbed up the manila folder, dashed into the bathroom to make sure his wet hair was still combed, and jumped into his truck and headed off for Martha's.

She was out on the landing at the top of the stairs, sprawled out in one of two canvas chairs that were new since his last visit. She waved him into the other one and asked him if he would like a drink. "Beer, or daiquiri, or . . ."

He wanted one of those cool green ones that looked like her eyes. "Daiquiri," he said, seeming to surprise her. As soon as she went inside he pulled at the damp circle that had already formed in the center of his back, where the truck seat had made contact with the cotton shirt.

She came back with two very good-looking drinks. She looked, Pete thought, very good herself, seeing her for the first time with arms and legs and shoulders and back clearly visible from around short-shorts and an insubstantial tank top. He sat in the canvas chair beside her and propped his sneakers up on the rail and began to feel . . . happy. He looked sideways at Martha, and she smiled. Was it possible that she was beginning to feel it too? They sipped silently for a moment, looking out over the harbor, and then Pete handed her the envelope he still held in his hand.

"This is a copy of the police report on your aunt's death. She was found in her boat; it was full of water and bashed up against the rocks, and since she was lying in the bottom of it, they of course at first assumed she had drowned. But in addition to the autopsy report with the alcohol and barbiturates, there was also a note. There's a copy of it in there. Seems funny to me that word of it never got around, but there you have it."

Pete looked away as Martha read the note. It was short, and already he had found himself unable to forget it.

Dear Edna,
Everything I do turns out wrong, but this I think is going to be the first thing I ever did just right. I know you never do anything wrong. I don't blame you. I love you. I just can't stand to sit around any more with nothing to do but watch.

Love, Lizzie

Martha shut the file. "I don't see anything funny about it," she said. "I'm sure my mother would have pulled whatever strings to hush it up. She would have hated everyone to know her sister killed herself."

"It's too bad," said Pete. "I can't help thinking that no matter what made her do it, if she'd just given it some time it would have worked out; she would have gotten over it." He was a little surprised to hear himself saying this. He *must* be happy, he thought.

They were silent for some time. "I wonder if anyone ever really gets over anything," said Martha, at last.

Pete looked over at her. "Not over it. But it works its way down into the grain so it becomes a part of you. You're never exactly the same as you were, but it's still the same piece of wood, if I could be so corny."

The same piece of wood. Pete looked out over the water and felt the first rustle of the evening breeze in his hair. It was nearing dusk, and a few car lights were now on over on the Hook, winking along the highway. Martha was making rummaging-around noises beside him, lifting her bare legs up from where they were sticking to the arm of the chair over which she had flung them, pulling at her tank top, which was sticking to her tightly. She got up.

"Another?" She picked up her own empty glass, and Pete downed the remainder of his and handed it over. He was sticking to the chair a little himself, and when she went inside he stood up and leaned against the balcony rail instead.

When she came back out she leaned against the rail beside him, so close that he could feel the heat coming off of her, could smell a nice clean soapy smell still whispering around her, but with the real smell of her skin and her hair coming through. She was very close, and he was beginning to wonder if it might not mean something, when she brushed his forearm with a finger.

"Are you a bisexual or an IV drug user?" she asked, and his glass slipped through his fingers and plowed into the sand a story below, not six inches from the feet of Police Chief Will McOwat.

The chief looked up at them. "No thanks," he said, "I'm on duty," and he plodded up the stairs to meet them. "It's convenient finding you both here," he continued. "At least for me it is. Saves me some work. No offense, Ms. Hitchcock, but you weren't my first choice. I stopped by your office, Pete, but you weren't there."

"He's here," said Martha, and the chief grinned.

"Thank you. May you continue to be so helpful."

Pete didn't say anything. He could feel Martha looking at him, but he didn't look at her face.

"Well!" The chief flipped open a notepad and turned more exclusively toward Pete. "Any relation to Constance B. Bartholomew, Pete?"

If his glass weren't already in the sand it would have been there now, thought Pete. "Not any more," he said.

"Exwife?"

Pete nodded.

"Would you happen to know where I could find her?"

"Why?" asked Martha, and both Pete and the chief turned to look at her.

"Because she was at your mother's house the night before she died," he answered, and this time Martha herself seemed to fumble with her glass.

"Why?" she asked again.

"Now if someone could tell me that, I would consider it extremely helpful," said the chief. Had he noticed that Pete was not particularly surprised? "Pete?"

"I don't know where she is," he answered. He

hoped the chief wouldn't notice he was running a question behind.

"I saw her at the Whiteaker," said Martha, and Pete whipped around and stared at her as hard as he could through the semidarkness.

The chief seemed to be surprised. He turned from Martha back to Pete. "When did you last speak with her, Pete?"

Pete was still looking at Martha. "I haven't," he said.

"You'll let me know if you do? Either of you?"

"Sure," said Martha.

"Thank you," said the chief. "And I'm sorry to have interrupted you. Good night." He descended the stairs and disappeared into the dark. The minute the Scout started up, Pete turned back to Martha.

"You saw her at the Whiteaker?"

"I was walking the beach." She pointed toward the sand, in the direction of the hotel. "She was out on the porch. I knew who she was from that day at Lupo's, at lunch."

"Why was she at your mother's?"

"Why don't you ask *her?*" Martha snapped.

Pete turned as if in a fog, obeying orders, starting down the steps. . . . Then he remembered something and stopped and turned. "No and no," he said. "To answer your previous questions."

"I'll keep that in mind."

"I'll let you know if there's any change?"

"Yes," she said, but she wasn't smiling, and she sounded . . . no longer very interested. Pete knew that if he stayed there was a chance he could do something about that, but all he wanted to do right then was to go down the stairs and over to the truck and go find Connie and tell her . . . tell her what? That the chief was on his way? Was he destined to spend the rest of his life with the wrong woman at the right time? Or was it the right woman at the wrong time?

"Martha," he said. He took a step up closer. "I have to go. You understand?"

"Yes," she said, but not as if she expected that, or cared if, he believed her.

Chapter
15

Pete pulled into the Whiteaker just as Willy's Scout was leaving, and the chief stopped as soon as they were driver's door to driver's door and spoke through the window.

"You called her?"

"Who?" asked Pete, not being obstructive, just feeling obtuse.

"Constance B. Bartholomew, that's who. You called her from Martha's?"

"No!" Pete looked up at the hotel. He wasn't sure, but he thought he saw Bill Freed's bulk just passing out of the lobby. He rubbed his forehead. This day had really been a little too much. This week. This year! "Are you trying to tell me she's gone?"

Willy McOwat stared at him hard for a few seconds. "Gone. Checked out. They don't know where. What are you doing here, Pete?"

Gone. So that was that. Pete waited for the inevitable relief to descend, but he felt . . . nothing. "I have no idea why I'm here," said Pete, "but since

I am, I'd like to tell you about some cars." He told him about the burgundy hatchback, and about Hardy Rogers, and, after some thought, he added the dark green car. The hardtop dark green car.

Rita was yawning. Not that anyone but Pete would have known she was yawning—her lips tightened down on each other and her nostrils flared ever so slightly—a very ladylike yawn, but a yawn all the same, a yawn that meant Rita had not gotten her usual ten hours of sleep the night before. She looked, if he really wanted to analyze the situation, as if she had just rolled out of somebody's bed that was not her own: Her hair was bent up in the back and one nail was chipped and her lipstick was on her desk, not on her mouth. She held a small mirror in one hand and looked over the top of it at Pete with a new look in her eye and continued to talk about Bill. Bill!

"I had no idea, of course, until he'd already moved out that that was what was going on. I mean, I knew he certainly was not himself of late, but I never thought it was because of that. Can you *imagine* it? I never in a million years ever dreamed that he would leave her. I mean, I know she's a bitch, but didn't you always think he really loved her? Didn't you? And that he'd actually get up the guts to really *go!* But he really has not been himself, haven't you noticed it? And today, well, he just couldn't seem to get a move on, you know what I mean? He's been moping around here for the past half hour, and I was kind of wondering if maybe he wanted to talk to you. Of course, if I'd known you were going to be so *late* . . . Maybe you should take him out for a drink or something, Pete. What do you think?''

"What did you do last night?'' Pete asked her, and sure enough, her face actually lit up with a wicked grin. He didn't wait to hear her answer; he left at once for Sarah's instead.

Talk about your wicked grins. Pete was hard pressed to decide whose was worse—Rita's or Sarah's. But he decided not to delve into what was behind Sarah's; sooner or later he would find out, and he had a feeling it would be plenty soon enough for him. He kissed her cheek, picked up the paper, and stretched out on the couch. "Acid Rain Claims Local Pond," he read.

He rambled on. Somewhere in the middle of the court report—Sarah's favorite part—he heard a car pull in and then pull out again.

Sarah frowned. "Who's that?''

Pete looked over his shoulder and could just see the tail end of the TR-6 as it left. He sat up. "Connie," he said. He looked at Sarah. "Doesn't seem to want to see me." Which was good, of course, but . . . Where did she go? he wondered.

Sarah's cane snapped hard onto the floor. "What's that damned fool up to? She said she'd be back by nine-thirty. Of course she wants to see you! She's going to see you and see you plenty. She lives here now."

Pete slid his legs onto the floor and sat up. "She's staying *here?*"

Sarah struggled to her feet and drew herself up to her tallest height. "I asked her. And she said yes. So what are you going to do about it?"

Pete looked at her. "Nothing, Sarah. But I'm not coming back here if Connie is—"

"So don't," snapped Sarah. "Last I looked, Connie could read."

Last I looked, Connie could read. Pete opened his mouth to say something hurtful, but he couldn't think of anything to equal that hurt that he would allow himself to say. "Good-bye, Sarah," he said instead.

Pete returned to Factotum. He called Rematch and registered Martha. He called Roberta Ballantine to make an appointment to discuss the Denault and Hitchcock families, but when she finally came on the phone she was uncooperative, to say the least. Pete stated his case and explained that he had written permission from Martha, the only remaining living relative, to discuss whatever she had in her files on the family, but Roberta Ballantine was not impressed.

"Mr. Bartholomew," she began, so that Pete knew it was no-go right off. "I don't care who has signed what. What this Ms. Hitchcock may know, she may tell you. What I know, I may not. Clear enough?"

"Could you at least tell me if you have records regarding the time in question, which would be . . ."

"No, I could not," she said, and she hung up the phone. Pete banged his own down somewhat forcefully and headed off to the dock to talk to Bob Wampeet.

It wasn't, at first, all that easy to get Bob to talk. It was eleven-thirty, the week before the Fourth, and the first summer visitors were in the hotel or on the beach and Bob knew they were getting ready to stroll up to his stand for lunch. He stood behind the counter, beefy forearms slamming hotdogs and packages of rolls into handy spots.

"Hey, Bob," said Pete.

"Hey, man." Bob kept moving.

"Got a couple of questions for you."

"Yeah?" A wad of grease slid across the grill.

"I hear you knew Lizzie Denault."

Bob raised his spatula for a minute and turned, then went back to chasing the grease. "Yeah? So?"

"I'm working for her niece, Martha Hitchcock. Looking into some stuff about the family. You and Lizzie used to date or something?"

The back of Bob Wampeet's neck expanded as he laughed. "Or something!"

"Meaning?"

Bob made a full turn and the spatula was raised a little too high above Pete's head for comfort. "So what the hell *is* this, Pete, huh? I got customers, y'know?"

"So if you don't want to help me just say so, dammit." Pete was feeling a little cranky himself by then, but the outburst seemed to do the trick. Bob grinned.

"Lizzie and I used to meet up in the shack on Gould's cranberry bog. I don't know about you, but I don't exactly call that dating."

Pete considered the various reasons you'd meet in a cranberry shack and decided it was safe to assume Bob Wampeet could have been the baby's father, except for one thing: His name wasn't Hal. "How long were you and Lizzie . . ."

135

Bob was now pounding the side of the Coke machine with a closed fist. He raised his voice. "Dunno. Summer. She met up with some guy from the base after that. I didn't see why she couldn't meet me in the shack when he wasn't around, but she said she didn't feel like it. Hell!" He laughed, and whatever he'd been trying to do to the Coke machine seemed to be done—he stopped banging.

Some guy from the base. Maybe this was going to be easy. "Do you remember the guy's name?"

Bob yanked his head left and right in a no, then looked up into the canvas over his head. "Wait. No. Dunno."

"Hal, maybe?"

Bob swung around and snapped his fingers in Pete's face. "Harold! That's it. Harold Stern. I remember I was some mad, I tell you." He swung back to the grill and rolled three hotdogs across it.

"Harold Stern," Pete repeated. "I don't suppose you know where he was from?"

"New York. Brooklyn, I think." His head was shaking again, left, right, left. "I told her! What do you want to hang out with someone from *Brooklyn* for? Jesus. But she wouldn't listen." He looked up and off at the water, and he shook his head again. "Blue eyes," he said. "She had these damnedest deep blue eyes. . . ." He looked pretty sad.

"I know this will sound like none of my business, Bob," Pete began, "but I don't suppose you'd know anything about Lizzie being pregnant?"

Bob turned fully around and narrowed his eyes at Pete. "Who wants to know, again?"

"Her niece. Martha. We're trying to keep track of the family. We're . . ."

Bob waved the rest of the sentence off. "She wasn't pregnant by me."

Pete wondered what he meant by that—whether he meant that things hadn't gone that far with Lizzie in the shack, or did he just mean that he had never given any thought to the possibility that she might have become pregnant from what they were doing in the shack and not have told him?

"She was pregnant?" Bob asked after a minute, frowning.

"Yes, she was. Somewhere between 1950 and 1953."

Bob looked up into the canvas again for some time, and when he looked back down again his face was clearer. "After me," he said, which again, could mean . . . what? Simply that he had no cause for retroactive jealousy? Or for retroactive guilt?

Bob turned back to the grill. A couple was moving down the dock toward the stand, and Pete was getting ready to move off himself, when Bob spoke again. His voice, echoing from the other side of the stand, was diffused, softer. "I heard she drowned. Then I heard just a while ago she didn't."

"No, she didn't."

"Ole Lizzie was a lot of fun," said Bob, still hunkered over the grill. "Real happy. At least she was at first. She got sadder later. Guess she never counted on life being so mixed up."

Tell me about it, thought Pete.

"She wanted everyone to be happy. Wanted to be friends with everybody, wanted everybody to like her. Always got real surprised when someone got hurt, you know.''

Pete said yes, he knew.

"I was real upset when I heard she drowned. I was real . . . mad, you know? I was married then and all, but still, I was real upset. Then all of a sudden, they start saying she killed herself, and it's a funny thing, but it made me feel better. She did what she wanted to do.'' Suddenly Bob Wampeet whirled around and flung a mustard jar into the wall at the end of the counter. The couple heading their way made a U-turn and started for the hotel lobby instead. Pete had one more question, but, under the circumstances, he decided it was best to slink away one answer short.

Harold Stern, from Brooklyn. Pete knew the Nashtoba library didn't stock New York phone books, since the Nashtoba librarian would never acknowledge the need for anyone to call New York. He set off for the Hook and the library in Bradford.

Bradford was the big city. It had the only hospital within sixty miles and the only chain hotels and the only real bus station and the only, although tiny, airport. Bradford always made Pete nervous— not because he wasn't comfortable driving around in its traffic, but because he was afraid that what he saw in Bradford was the future of his own little island, of the rest of the Hook. . . . He tried to drive by the hospital without looking—*that* place really did make him nervous—and tend to his business at the library as quickly as he could. There were traffic lights in Bradford. *Traffic lights!* And three rotaries. Pete was as fast as he could be, but it was thirty miles each way, so it was late when he got back from Bradford with his Stern listings, too late to call any of them.

But was it too late to call Martha? The phone rang ten times, but Pete held on, convincing himself that the information gleaned from Bob Wampeet and his six phone numbers would be worth it to Martha if she would only wake up.

She did. "It's very late," said Pete, "but I couldn't help thinking that you'd like to hear. The Hal in the letter is Harold Stern, in Brooklyn, and there are still two Harold Sterns listed there and four H. Sterns. I'll be calling them in the morning, but I . . . I wanted to tell you this much tonight."

"Thank you," said Martha.

Keep talking, please.

Silence.

Pete tried to think of something—anything—to keep her on the phone.

"Rita and John Clark have asked me out to dinner on Saturday. They said you were going. Are you going?"

"I don't know," said Martha.

He babbled on, fast. "It's the Fourth. At the Whiteaker. Because you can see the fireworks from there, from the tables on the porch. Have you ever done that?"

"No," said Martha. There was a minute's silence, and then she cleared her throat, and Pete felt that he could see her sitting up from under her covers in bed, wearing . . . what would she be wearing? A T-shirt, he figured.

"I feel it only fair to warn you," she said, "that I think they're trying to fix us up."

Silence. Pete was no good at this, no good at this at all. "Maybe we could beat them to it," he said finally, and he was embarrassed to feel his heart begin to slam into his chest. This was getting ridiculous. "For example," he charged on, "maybe tomorrow we could—"

"I can't tomorrow," she answered, fast. "I . . . have to clean out my mother's house."

And in a flash, all the pain and fear that he could hear behind her words put his own adolescent worrying clear out of his head. "I could help you," he said, despite the fact that as much as he knew she didn't want to go back to that house, he didn't want to go back to it even more.

He couldn't have been more surprised when, after another lengthy and unreadable pause, she said, "All right."

"I'll pick you up."

"No," said Martha. "I'll meet you there at ten."

"I'll be there," he said. And then he said, "Good night, Martha," and he hung up the phone before he did something to wreck it.

Hardy Rogers stared across his desk at the cops—two of them, this time. Paul Roose wouldn't look him in the eye and the chief wouldn't stop looking at him, and Hardy was having a hard time trying to decide which of the two of them was more annoying.

"Let's start this once again," said the chief.

Hardy hated it when people did that. If you didn't get it the first time around, what made you think it was going to sink into your thick head any better the next?

"Edna Hitchcock called you to come out to her

house on a house-call basis? For medical reasons?"

Hardy exploded. "Christ on a raft! What other reasons do you think I'd be going out there for!"

"On Sunday?"

"*Yes,* on Sunday. This isn't the city here."

"And on other occasions as well?"

Hardy remained silent and looked at them.

"We have received information that on several occasions you had gone out to Mrs. Hitchcock's house—"

"All right all right all right. Like as not, if she called me I came. The woman was crazy." Hardy thought a minute and amended that. "Not crazy. Sick. She was sick. I'm the one who was nuts, thinking I'd do any good for that screwball family in the first place." He started thinking, again, of Martha. Was it any wonder that she turned out a little strange? Didn't nuts fall close to the tree?

"Edna would call with some cooked-up reason, and I'd go out and it would be nothing. So shoot me for a sucker." He leaned back in his chair. "Will that be all?"

"There was never any real medical reason for your presence?"

"Can't recall a one. Usually just needed an ear to holler in about . . ." Usually it was about Martha, but Hardy thought better about naming names. He stopped talking.

"And on the Sunday before her death it was much the same?"

"Yes."

"What did she give you as the reason for the call?"

"Said she fell and hurt her hip and couldn't move. I went out—"

"Why?"

"Jesus, Mary, and Joseph! How many times do I—"

"Why would you go out on a Sunday, to see a woman who was no longer a patient, who had, according to your own words, fired you some weeks before?"

There really wasn't what you could call a good answer for that, so Hardy said nothing at all.

Chapter
16

Pete came through the hall into the Factotum part
of his cottage at eight in the morning and was surprised to see Rita already sitting at her desk. She
had been arriving later, of late, and absenting herself earlier, and, as a matter of fact, lunch seemed
to be stretching out. . . .

"When you get back from Sarah's—" she
began, but he interrupted her.

"I won't be going to Sarah's."

Now Rita was the one to look surprised, but she
didn't let it slow her down much; she saw a window of opportunity and she took it. "Good. Then
you should have time to go over those applications
that have been sitting on your desk for—"

Pete waved a hand. "I've got some important
calls to make."

"I'll make the calls."

"Not these calls." He strode toward his office
door but then stopped halfway, turned around, and
looked at Rita. He crossed back over to her desk
and sat on his usual spot on its corner, realizing it

had been a while since he last sat there, had been a while since a lot of things: lunch, real conversation . . . It felt good to sit there. He smiled. Rita stopped frowning at once and smiled back.

"I think I'm close to Hal," he said. "I hope I'm close to Hal. I found out his name and I have six possibilities in the Brooklyn phonebook. I want to call them before I meet Martha at ten." He looked at his watch. "I'm going to help her clean out her mother's house."

Somewhere along the line, Rita had started to frown again.

"Pete," she began. She reached out a hand and touched his wrist. "Do you ever wonder if maybe Martha . . . if maybe Martha *did* do something to her mother?"

Pete leaned down and peered into Rita's face. "Don't tell me you've been listening to gossip."

"It's not gossip. It's—"

"Aw, Rita. Of course she didn't do anything to her mother. Even Willy is off that now." I think, thought Pete. I hope. He outlined a few of the other leads the police were now tracking down. He told Rita that he expected Martha for dinner on the Fourth, expecting her to be pleased, knowing that he had not exactly been enthusiastic about this John Clark clown, hoping that this would show Rita that he didn't mind . . . but Rita's frown was deeper.

He slid off her desk.

"Read those aps!" she hollered after him. Love didn't seem to be agreeing with her of late.

Once in his "office," he shoved the wheelbarrow out of the way and sat down at his desk, stretching his hands out flat on the pile of papers in front of him. He sighed. He had bought this particular desk because he loved the look and feel of aged wood, and because it was so big that he was sure there would always be room for however many books or papers or coffee cups he needed to store on it; but he had since learned that there was no such thing as enough desk. He had piled everything on the peripheral edges and worked in from there until once again he was left with a square foot of space, and that only after he had shoved the Sunday paper on top of the employment applications. He had made several attempts at really sitting down there to read them. He would start reading, sorting into yes, no, and maybe piles the efforts of Rita's hard work; then he would look over the desk to make sure there wasn't something more important he should be reading, such as the sports page or the takeout menu from the Ling Garden. Then he'd look back at the three piles and apply the Sarah Abrew Test, and the next thing he knew, the one yes became a definite no and he really couldn't quite call those two maybes real maybes. Then he'd swing his chair around the other way to check the Sound for whitecaps, and just about then he would discover he had to be somewhere else all of a sudden, like the bathroom, or Beston's porch.

Pete shuffled around on the desk until he found the phone listings for the Sterns. He pulled the phone close and began to dial. No answer at the first Harold Stern. He dialed the second one and a woman answered. "Hello," began Pete. He identified himself as Factotum, a research company on Cape Hook. May God forgive me, he said to himself, but no one from Brooklyn would ever have heard of Nashtoba. He explained he was doing some work on a family tree, and he asked if this were the home of Harold Stern.

"*Who's* this?"

Pete began again. He was trying to locate a Harold Stern, who had been in the Air Force and had once been stationed at the Bradford base.

"Hal's dead," said the woman, "and I don't know what it is you think you wanted out of him."

"I'm sorry," said Pete. "I didn't realize. I see now that . . ." Yes, it was as Martha had suspected: Hal had never come back. "We had come across a letter he had written from Korea," he explained.

"Ko-*ree*-a! I don't think this is very funny, young man. He died in the middle of the Pacific Ocean in 1944; he wasn't in any Korea."

"I'm sorry," said Pete again. "I think I have the wrong number." He hung up the phone.

Behind him he could hear children's voices cutting in and out from the beach across the marsh. An outboard whined. A breeze caught the window and hit the back of his neck, and the breeze felt hot already. He looked at his watch, wondering if he'd have time for a swim before he met Martha. He dialed the first H. Stern and found that his phone had been disconnected. No answer at the second. The child who answered at the third said his parents weren't up yet and hung up on him. The fourth H. Stern was home, but his name was Hubert. There were no Harolds in his family tree.

Pete sighed. He pulled the employment applications over in front of him and he would have begun reading them, but just then he heard voices in the hall. He opened his door and peeked out.

There were two of them. They were talking to Rita, and one of them was laughing and the other was looking at Rita with a remoteness in her eyes that reminded Pete of Martha. The laughing one was saying to Rita, "Oh, no, our mother never lets us dress alike. She says it denies our individual identities. And we had different hair till I cut all Bentley's off."

"Car," said Bentley, and she pointed at the door in which Pete was standing.

Pete moved forward. Once the laughing one stopped laughing he couldn't tell them apart, and he didn't know what the heck they were going on about over the clothes, since they were dressed in identical Sid Vicious T-shirts and cut-off jeans. He looked from one freckled face to the other, at one set of short red curls to the other, and turned to stare at Rita.

"Please meet our two newest employees," Rita said. "Carlisle and Bentley Brown, this is Peter Bartholomew."

Pete opened his mouth at Rita, but she held up her hand. "I mean it," she said. "I mean I've had it. You have to admit that your own hiring record is not too hot, and if I have to wait around one more day for you to settle on some Sarah Abrew—"

"Pleased to meet you both," Pete interceded, and he held out his hand.

"Pleased to meet you," repeated the laughing twin, Carlisle Brown. Bentley Brown said nothing at all.

"Don't worry about a thing," said Rita. "Bill and I will train them. Now you go do your phoning."

Pete scratched his head and looked at the twins, and now that neither was smiling again he had his doubts as to which had been which. "You say you don't usually dress the same?"

Carlisle grinned again. "Well, yes, I know, but sometimes it's fun, like if we're applying for a job or something. We just sneak out of the house and change up in the car."

Twins. Teenage twins. Flaky teenage twins. What would Sarah think? Then Pete remembered that he no longer much cared what Sarah thought, might very well not be seeing her for a while. Then he remembered something else: He wasn't going to have to face that pile of applications. He was free!

"I think I'll go for a swim," he said to Rita.

"Fine," said Rita.

Pete stared at her. She actually seemed to *mean* it. Was he the only crazy one, or was it everybody else?

He threw on his shorts and jumped in the truck and headed toward the Point, bypassing the calmer marsh waters where he usually swam, heading for the heavier surf. He needed to churn things around a bit, to see if things came out more right side up once he was upside down in a wave. He knew a secret place that he had shared with Connie: It wasn't where the surfers went; it was just off Shore Road a few hundred yards before The Spookhouse, a sandy spit in between scrub pines that led down over some rocks to a beach with a nice high sandbar that broke the waves way out and rolled them all the way in. He would have time to swim, and then he'd go straight to Martha's.

He pulled into the secret place and swore. There were two cars there ahead of him. Big secret! Pete parked as far off into the trees as he could and cut through the woods to an empty stretch of beach and plunged out through the surf and into the water. He bucked through the waves, suddenly wanting not to ride them, but to fight against them, to beat the water, to swim. He struck out horizontally to the shore once he was past the breakers and settled into a slow crawl, but something on fire inside him began to pound into the water harder and harder, his arms and shoulders shoveling the water with fury. Sound and fury. Signifying . . . something. When he finally quit it was not because he was tired, but because it wasn't working.

He beat Martha there. When the VW pulled up, he got out of the truck and walked up the porch steps beside her, neither of them speaking at all. He counted the creaks—one, two, three. There were two locks; one was so old it took a key that looked like something Ben Franklin might have strung up in his kite; the other was a Yale. Martha cranked the older key first, then put the Yale key in the lock . . . and she rested her head against the painted door and closed her eyes. Pete laid a hand on her shoulder. She pushed herself away from the door, jabbed at the newer, brighter lock, and nothing happened. Pete heaved a shoulder against the warped door; it swung open, and they went in.

There was a definite funk to the air.

"I guess we start with the kitchen," said Martha, and she led the way through an archway to the right, across a dining room full of heavy mahogany furniture that seemed to suffocate the air. Or was it that smell from the kitchen?

On a pine table in front of a bay window in the kitchen was a vase full of dead lilacs, and Martha crossed at once and scooped up the vase and carried it over to the sink. She shook the brown stems out of the jar and opened a bottom cupboard where the wastebasket was, and they were hit with a wave of foulness so stiff that she had to back halfway across the kitchen. Garbage. How long had it been there? Long enough. Pete picked the bag out of the basket, tied it off, set it out on the porch, and left the door open to air. When he returned to the kitchen, Martha had opened the windows and set some cardboard boxes out on the floor. What next? She crossed the blue-and-white ceramic tiles to the refrigerator and opened the door, and Pete went with her. There was almost nothing in the refrigerator. Moldy cream cheese. Sour milk. Frozen dinners in the freezer. Martha grabbed a box of garbage bags from under the sink and began to throw everything out, frozen dinners and all. She moved toward the cupboards and began firing their contents into the bags: flour, sugar, tea, cans of coffee. Everything on the shelves and on the counters was lined up in neat, graduated rows, right down to the magnetic knife rack with the small vegetable peeler at one end, the heavy blade of the meat knife at the other. Martha flung things onto the floor, hitting and missing the garbage bag and not caring. She was crying, throwing things in with the garbage, things that didn't belong, things like a double boiler.

Pete came up behind her and took hold of her firmly. He took a pan out of her hand and set it on the counter and pulled her up to face him. She was still crying, but she seemed to be going with it, letting him hold her . . . No. Wrong. She wasn't. She twisted out of his arms and stopped crying, raking the tears off her face, and Pete could almost see the force of her will as she regained her own control and then went on from there to controlling the rest of the situation, calling it the way she wanted it. No, she wasn't going to be sobbing into his chest and letting him comfort her. She didn't look at him. She grabbed onto the short hair at the nape of his neck and kissed him on the mouth, then on the jaw, then on the neck, sinking lower. She kissed him where the hair was on his chest and she kissed him where it wasn't and she kissed him where it started to appear again. . . . He tried to stop her, but not for long.

He was having some trouble assimilating. First there they were—on the kitchen *floor,* for God's sake—and Martha was lying flushed and sweaty on top of him; and then the next thing he knew she was up, collecting her clothes, pulling on her T-shirt and getting her toes caught in her underpants. She rounded the doorway into the dining room and returned with several bottles of wine and began to shove them into one of the boxes, resuming her chores. Pete wasn't too crazy about wine, but he knew enough about it to recognize an expensive Bordeaux as it went by into the box, and he felt an odd kind of wincing pain as she crammed Tupperware in around it. Tupperware! He raised himself onto one elbow and stared at her. What the hell was going on here? She picked up a glass from the counter and dropped it, and as it shattered she started to cry again. Pete got up and lifted her and her bare feet out of the glass and set her down on the kitchen chair. Then he pulled on his shorts and began to sweep up the glass.

"Peter Bartholomew," he said. "Factotum. A person employed to do all kinds of work." When he looked over at her, she was staring at the knives on the wall, her eyes dry again, her face stiff and cold.

"No charge," he added. He swept the glass up and into a plastic bag, returned to the table, and leaned against it beside her. "What do you think, enough of this for today?"

Martha seemed to snap out of it. "Yes," she said. "Please. I . . . I think you should go. I just need to be alone here for a minute. . . ."

Pete pushed away from the table. "Fair enough. I'll call you later?"

"Yes. Please." After a second she said, "Thank you," but it wasn't exactly clear for what. For leaving? He kissed her and left the house, picking up the bag of stinking garbage off the porch and throwing it in the back of his truck to take to the dump on the next run.

He went home to change and then drove back to the Point, planning to stop in on Henry Baker, maybe check in on Martha on the way, but her car was gone by the time he drove by the house. As he headed on toward Henry's, he started worrying about that later call he had promised to make to Martha. What would he say? He should ask her out, but what would they do? He was thirty-six years old and he was lousy at dating. He had never once liked it, and he couldn't quite believe that it was something he was going to have to start doing again. Anything normal he thought of seemed too . . . normal: eating out, a movie, a play in Bradford. Anything else seemed too corny, too affected, too something-out-of-a-1940s-movie. He could suggest a midnight swim—he immediately thought of *From Here to Eternity*—and canned that. Or a walk up the Indian Tower. You could see all the lights on the Hook from there—even the bridge over to the mainland from the Hook that was like a string of pearls on velvet at night. . . . That's just what I mean, he said to himself: You think of the Indian Tower and you get corny. What he really wanted to do was to go back to the boathouse or have her come back to his cottage, where they could sit on the porch for a while and talk and . . . But what if he said that? She would think he wanted to screw. Not that he didn't! But he didn't want her to think that was the only reason he wanted to see her. *Would* she think that? At their ages, weren't you past all that? It had been her idea this first time; it should be his idea the next. If she didn't want to, she would say she didn't want to, wouldn't she? Why had none of this ever been a problem with Connie? But he was going to have to stop thinking about Connie. He slammed shut the Connie portion of his brain, willing Martha's image back to the front, but the image that came to him was one of her face as she sat staring at the knives as he cleaned up the glass— not exactly the romantic image he was looking to find. He shivered. So who said love was perfect?

You did, you idiot, he answered. Once.

Chapter
17

Sarah was driving Connie crazy. First it was the fight over the peanut butter.

"Jif!" hollered Sarah. "What's this Jif!"

"Peanut butter," said Connie.

"Skippy," said Sarah, "is the only peanut butter that's edible. *Skippy.*"

"You're never too old to change," said Connie, and then Sarah had really blown her top.

"You think you're so smart, don't you? Don't you? No wonder Pete got fed up. Jif! It won't take him long to do better, you mark my words."

"He's welcome to do better or worse, for all I care," said Connie, and she started to edge toward the door; but edging toward the door at Sarah's could take quite a long time, she had learned.

"You *say* that, Connie Bartholomew, but you don't mean it. I happen to have a few sources that say he won't be loose for long."

"Martha Hitchcock again, right?" said Connie,

intending to go on from there about how little she cared, but Sarah's head came up with a snap.

"So who told you that?"

Connie gave up on the door and turned the corner for the kitchen instead. Sarah followed. "Nobody. It just figures, is all. Spending all this time looking for this long-lost cousin, her mother dead and all, he'll start feeling sorry for her and then next thing you know . . ." Connie rummaged around in the cupboard and got down a box of Wheaties.

"You're not eating again!"

"I'm hungry." She filled a bowl and began to peel a banana.

Sarah sat down at the kitchen table. "In two weeks you'll be as fat as a house. I don't recall you ever being hungry all the time like this."

Connie paused around a mouthful to say, "I wasn't," but she decided to let it go at that.

"The trouble with Martha Hitchcock," said Sarah, "is that she never learned to take responsibility for her own actions. *What* cousin?"

Connie explained the general gist that had been drifting around the island ever since Pete had talked to Bob Wampeet. Once she was through with the Wheaties, she decided to have herself a bagel.

"What in the world are those things?"

"Bagels, Sarah."

Sarah pounded the table once with the flat of her hand. "I won't have it!" she said. "I want this foreign food out of my house!" Her hand was actually shaking.

Connie in all her life had never seen anyone so upset about a bagel.

*　　*　　*

Pete knew Henry Baker. He and his sister Polly had ventured as far around the Point as Henry Baker's house once or twice, and more recently Factotum had reshingled his roof. He remembered the roof and the house under it with affection: The house was Victorian, white, surrounded by so many pines that the lawn was all needles. He remembered Henry Baker with affection also. He was a contemporary of Sarah's, but he did not fit into the Nashtoba–Sarah Abrew–Hardiman Rogers mold; a gentler man had rarely lived. His skin was the wrinkled leather of any eighty-year-old who spent most of his time out of doors, his head bald and so speckled with old-age spots that it looked like a large bird's egg. When Pete reintroduced himself at the door, Henry Baker waved him right in, and his smile was neither the fury-filled one of Brenda Hayes nor the suspicion-riddled one of Muriel Hatch. It was refreshing.

Henry Baker's living room was a mix of old Victorian and new comfort: An oval, marble-topped table was making marks in a synthetic magenta carpet; there was a color TV on a gate-legged table and a Jack Higgins mystery on the caned footstool. Pete picked up the mystery and sat on the stool, since Henry Baker had sat in the only other spot not occupied by a cat, and explained his business.

"I'd be happy to talk to you about the Denault family, Pete. Not much left of 'em now, of course."

"No." Pete looked at his notebook as if it held prepared questions and waited for Henry Baker to comment further on Edna's death or Martha's escapades. He did not.

"I'm especially interested in Lizzie Denault, Edna's sister."

"Poor Lizzie," said Henry, and Pete exhaled. Finally someone who had actually known her.

"Now let's see," began Henry. "I first met the girls when Mary, their mother, began coming down summers with them to the house. Arthur was a lawyer up on Beacon Hill and he didn't get down so much. Now, in those days, of course, there wasn't the Hayes house between us the way it is now, and the girls thought nothing of the distance. They'd run down the beach to play with my daughter Roberta."

A small lightbulb was flickering off and on in Pete's brain, but it failed to illuminate anything.

"They'd climb up the steps in front of my house and feed the catbirds. It was mostly Roberta and Edna who were friends; Roberta was the oldest. Funny." He stopped talking.

Pete waited.

"Y'know, Edna and Roberta were the real friends, but then it was Edna stopped coming around first. Those girls went off to school, see, and got to be teenagers, and teenagers don't like to hang around old people. Lizzie still came, though. Would you like a cup of tea?"

"No, thank you though," said Pete.

"Now, Lizzie was a real live wire. I swear, half the time she was hiding out over here when Mary and Arthur wanted her somewhere else, but Celie and I decided not to make any fuss over it. Keep your nose out of it, I always say." That, too, struck Pete as refreshing. Henry Baker chuckled. "Course, the other half the time I think Lizzie told 'em she was here when she wasn't!" He chuckled again and then grew instantly solemn. "I hardly saw Edna at all in recent years, but still, I can't quite believe them gone. Not both of them. I didn't much drop my teeth about Lizzie; she was always accident prone anyway, always taking chances, out in every kind of gale and taking the road past my house in some boy's car doing forty. Edna, though, she never put a foot wrong. Never once . . ." He shook his head. "Course, now I hear all this business about Lizzie not having drowned after all." His eyes bore into Pete's all of a sudden. "Didn't she?"

"No," said Pete.

Henry Baker sighed and seemed to be all done. Pete cleared his throat and prompted him along.

"You say Edna never put a foot wrong?"

Henry shook his head again. "I almost felt sorry for her at one time, always so worried about how she looked, what she said, who she was with. . . . Then after she had that little one and it all came down on her head, I started feeling . . ." He stopped and looked around him, as if for a new topic. His eyes must have lighted upon one on the table against the wall. "Would you care for a glass of sherry? I don't suppose it's exactly the right time. . . ."

Sherry. What wouldn't he be drinking next? "That would be nice," said Pete, and Henry Baker hopped up with surprising nimbleness and grabbed the decanter in one fist and two tiny glasses in the other. He poured out two glasses of sherry, raised his own up to his eyes, said, "Here's looking at you!" and tossed an undetectable amount of it away. Pete took a judicious sip of his own and noticed that the glass was nearly empty. Henry promptly refilled it. Pete wondered how Henry Baker had gotten along with the chief.

"How *is* Martha?" asked Henry. "She doing all right?"

Pete considered the question seriously and answered it as accurately as he felt able, the wild gamut of scenes in her mother's kitchen flooding his mind. "As well as can be expected under the circumstances," he said.

Henry Baker seemed to be giving him a shrewd once-over.

Pete looked down at his empty notebook. "You knew Martha well?" It wasn't what he was supposed to be asking.

"Not well. No, maybe after all, I did know her as well as most; she didn't have much in the way of friends. Maybe that's why she liked to come here."

"Martha came here, too?"

"Yup. Loved those catbirds—they'd eat right out of your hand, see? But Martha was timid. Serious. Funny girl. I mean, not that she didn't have a sense of humor, don't get me wrong!" Henry's sherry was sitting on the glass-topped coffee table, looking untouched. Pete's was already gone. Henry lifted the bottle, and Pete covered the top of his glass. He was going to have to start watching this drinking business.

"She was so serious I used to make a point of getting her laughing. I'd tell her these stories, some crazy thing about what someone was up to or something, and if it was funny—really funny—she'd get laughing away good. She was no pushover, though; it couldn't be just silly, it had to be clever, and if it wasn't, she'd just stand there and look at me all disappointed and wait for me to tell one right." He chuckled. "She kept me on my toes, all right! Then *she* became a teenager. She was a pretty little thing—still was, last time I saw her. . . ." He stopped talking and peered, again, at Pete. "But you don't want to hear about Martha. Where did we leave off about Lizzie?"

Pete was embarrassed to be reminded of what he had really come here for. Still, there was one point he couldn't let go by just yet. "Mr. Baker, could you back up just for a minute? You said a bit ago that it all came down on Martha's head. I'd be interested to know exactly what you meant by that."

Again, the shrewd look. He picked up his sherry glass, and Pete noticed for the first time that Henry's hand was trembling slightly. "I don't mean to say I'm an expert on raising girls, don't get me wrong. But I know a little about human nature and a whole lot about common sense. And I suppose I didn't get the whole picture, since Martha sure as heck never said anything, but I'm an old beachcomber and I've been downwind once too often with the voices going at gale force, and I'm telling you, Edna Hitchcock had two ways of treating that girl: One was to pretend she didn't exist, and the other was to accuse her of things before she even knew how to do them. Martha tried for a long time to please that woman, and I for one am not going to blame her for finally giving up." Henry then jumped up off his chair and disappeared, returning with a lumpy ceramic container painted with wobbly blue stripes. "Martha made this for her mother. She was nine years old. *Nine*. She was pretty darned proud of it, and she brought it over here to show me before she gave it to her mother. I fussed over it like any normal human being would do; it was to go on her mother's stove for the cooking spoons, and the blue stripes matched the tiles in her kitchen."

Pete was suddenly reminded of those blue tiles and what had happened on them last. He picked up the sherry glass and tossed off the last drops to hide his expression.

"Martha gave it to her mother," said Henry, "and two weeks later she found it out in the tool shed under all the junk. She brought it over to me because I'd said how much I liked it." Henry put down the jug so hard that everything on the table rattled. "But you didn't want to talk about Martha?" This time it was a question.

Pete cleared his throat. "No, I didn't. I'm here because it turns out that Lizzie had a baby. Martha hired me to see if I could find out what happened to it. Any ideas?"

Henry Baker blinked. "Lizzie didn't have any baby. How'd she get that idea?"

Pete explained, then asked, "Would you happen to remember any friends of Lizzie's? Boyfriends or girlfriends who might know more about it?"

Henry Baker continued to stare at him. "You could talk to my daughter Roberta," said Henry. "But she certainly never said anything to me about it if she knew."

"Roberta . . ." Pete's lightbulb started up again.

"Roberta Ballantine, the lawyer," said Henry with pride.

161

The lawyer who could not talk about her clients. But a *friend* could . . .

Pete returned to Factotum and, after one and a half hours, managed to get Roberta Ballantine back on the phone. He didn't get much out of her, but he did get her to agree to see him on Friday, which was enough.

Chapter
18

In the end they decided on clam fritters on the dock. It wasn't corny, and as far as Pete could recollect, there were no 1940s movies in which clam fritters played a feature role.

He met her at the boathouse, and when she came to the door he actually took a step back from her to take a longer look. She looked terrific. She was wearing a cotton skirt and a cropped white blouse, and she had had an afternoon in the sun: There was a dusty peach sunburn on her nose and cheeks, and her hair had done the same thing Connie's did in the sun—instead of pale brown it had now turned gold in places around her face and in long streaks down to the ends. It threw him, for a minute, that hair—the thought that she had even for a second reminded him of Connie. Did she really? Connie's eyes were sometimes deeper green. Connie's face was never still. Connie was much taller, Connie was . . . Pete shook his head. They were, really, nothing alike. Not really.

They left their shoes at the boathouse and

walked down the beach to the dock, and Pete discovered he wasn't the only one who had been thinking about Connie.

"I was wondering if you talked to your wife," Martha began. "I was curious as to why she would have been at my mother's."

"I haven't talked to her."

"She wasn't at the hotel?"

"She'd gone," said Pete, and he looked at Martha and suddenly felt there was something wrong with that answer. "That's not to say that I went there to find her. I don't know why I went there. . . ."

Martha held up a pale hand against the dark. "I would like to know why she went there. To my mother's. Will you be speaking with her? Do you know where she is?"

Pete considered. He weighed a few things and decided this was something a thousand dollars didn't include. He did not want to see Connie. "I know that she's staying at Sarah Abrew's, but no, I won't be speaking with her." He could feel Martha looking at him as they walked. He had said it a little too forcefully, perhaps?

They didn't speak for some time. They walked side by side in the sand toward the lights of the dock and the Whiteaker Hotel, their shoulders touching now and then. They ordered their clam fritters, walked up the road to Luke's for a couple of beers, and returned to the dock to eat. Pete forgot about *From Here to Eternity*. He forgot how corny the Indian Tower was supposed to be, and he began to tell Martha about it: how it was called the Indian Tower, but it was really the pilgrims who'd built it to keep watch for Indian attacks—

which made no sense, since until they built the tower the Indians had been perfectly friendly. Martha hadn't known that. She seemed interested, and they decided to go there some time, but not tonight. Tonight Martha suggested they go back to the boathouse, and Pete couldn't remember what was supposed to be wrong about that. They finished their beers, he reached down to pull her up off the dock and kept hold of her hand. They walked, again in silence, back to the boathouse.

Once inside, the mood changed.

"I'd like to show you something," said Martha. She moved into the living room, snapped on the light, picked up some papers from the barrel, and sat down on the cot.

Pete blinked in the light, returned to earth, and sat down beside her.

One of the papers he recognized. It was the copy of Lizzie's suicide note. He began to read the other one. It was a portion of a letter, a second half page:

. . . told us you give him not one single reason for this decline in your grades. Your father and I have discussed this with Bart Holmes and we have decided that you will stay for a summer session and try to rectify this situation. Failing that, it will be back to Oakes in the fall. They were not anxious to take you after your past performance there, but your father has prevailed upon them to do so. It is now up to you. If you do not want to return to Oakes you had best apply yourself this summer.

Love, Mother

Martha seemed used enough to the content to be able to move right on. She pointed to the word "you" in the "Love, Mother" letter and the same word in the suicide note. "What do you think?"

Pete looked at her.

"They were written years apart, I know that, but this was the best I could do. Don't they seem similar to you?"

Pete looked again. There was something . . . related, he had to admit that; but then again, so were the two people. "You're thinking what, Martha?"

"The police made an effort to verify this note as my aunt's actual handwriting. But who do you suppose would have supplied them with the samples of it?"

Pete began to feel nervous.

Martha folded one foot up underneath her and twisted to face him. "Well? Don't you see? What if my mother wrote both? What if she killed my aunt, just the way someone killed her? She could have written that note and then provided her own written samples in the guise of Lizzie's papers."

"But why?"

Martha looked away. "I have no idea why. But don't you agree the same person wrote both these notes?"

Pete was silent for a long time. He didn't agree. And he was starting to get very worried about Martha. Again.

"Did you rectify the situation?" he asked finally, with a smile, but Martha frowned back.

"I don't know what you mean."

"The grades. Was it Oakes in the fall, or . . ."

"Oh, that." Martha got up and walked over to the archway leading into the bedroom. "They shipped me back to Oakes, but I didn't rectify them there, either.''

"Why not?"

"It seemed so obvious at the time." She laughed, but not as if anything were funny. "If I flunked out of them all, I thought I'd get to come home.''

"Couldn't you just tell them—"

"No," said Martha. "I couldn't." She was still in the archway, still facing away from him.

Pete got up and stood behind her and wrapped an arm around her neck, but she pushed him away and returned to the cot to pick up the two letters.

"Could you at least do this for me?"

At least? And what was that in reference to?

"Would you take these to the chief and ask him about it? Ask him if he could have them analyzed or whatever it is that they do. You're on better terms with him than I am.''

And what was *that* in reference to? Had she somehow gotten wind of his talks with Willy and was she now assuming he was in the enemy camp? Well, that was one thing that was easy enough to straighten out. "Listen, Martha . . .''

Martha walked past him into the bedroom, looked at her alarm clock, and came back out. "I have to go," she said. "I've got to meet someone. Do you mind?''

"Yes," said Pete. "What the hell is this? I'll show Willy the letters, but I'd like you to talk to me for one minute.''

Martha looked scared to death. That was the only way Pete could possibly describe it: scared to death.

"I can't. Not now, please. Tomorrow, all right?"

"Martha . . ." He grabbed her arm and she tore it away.

"Please!"

"All right, all right. Tomorrow. When?"

"I'll call you tomorrow and we'll set it all up." She thrust the letters into his hands. She took hold of his face and kissed him. She threw a lot into it, but somehow Pete would have felt a lot better if she hadn't done it at all.

Rita looked down the length of her stockinged leg at the man at her feet, and said, "What?"

The man at her feet looked up the leg and into her eyes and repeated, "Would you like me to rub your feet?"

It was true. John Clark was down on one knee of his dress slacks, his pink shirt was unbuttoned at the neck, and his tie was untied. He slid one hand up the underside of her leg until he got to the top of her stocking and gently lifted her with the other hand and peeled off her hose. He began to massage her right foot.

"You were saying?" he prompted.

What *had* she been saying? She'd told him about the new twins and they had laughed and she had felt very amusing. Her description of Pete's face had been quite good, she thought. It was so much fun to feel entertaining, witty, sexy, instead of organized, caring, dull—all the things she felt around Pete. Pete. That's what she'd been saying. The murder. She leaned back and closed her eyes. "Well, I really can't believe that man sometimes. He doesn't have a distrustful bone in his body. I mean, here *everyone* knows she and her mother hated each other's guts. And she really can be very cold. At first I thought how nice it would be if they got together. I mean, the man hasn't *looked* at another woman since his wife left. And not that he hasn't had the chance! There's this woman, Elaine Carroll: She's had Factotum over there with every excuse under the sun, and does he take the hint? No, of course not. And now who does he decide to pick on? The one person on the whole island practically accused of murder. I wouldn't mind so much if I felt he was capable of a little healthy mistrust. You'd think he'd have learned a lesson by now about trusting people, wouldn't you?"

"Yes, I would," said John Clark. He began to massage her other foot. "But you seem awfully mistrustful of this Martha person yourself. You wouldn't, I suppose, be the least little bit jealous?"

Rita sat up. "Of course not. If anyone's the least little bit jealous, it's *him*. You should see what happens to his face whenever *your* name comes up. He even asked me one day if I was completely sure you weren't married! Now, if he'd only apply a little of that skepticism to some others I could name . . . And the more I see of her, the more I feel she's not his type. He's caring, she's cold."

John finished with the left foot and slid two hands up to her calf. "Cold?"

"When her father died, she didn't even come to his funeral."

John checked himself and straightened briefly. "Her father . . . died too?"

"He wasn't murdered or anything, if that's what you mean. Although there are some who say his wife did cause it!"

"But surely," said John, "the daughter can't be the only person the police are questioning. Surely there must be someone else upon whom suspicion has been cast, an old lover or a—"

"Old lover! Not her! She was as puritanical as you can get." It was fun, thought Rita, to be able to say that and know that she would not be apt to be included in those ranks. But still, thought Rita, didn't she recall a rumor once? It was a thought worth pursuing, and she *would* pursue it, but some other time. John Clark's hands had reached her thigh.

"I'll call you tomorrow," Martha had said, and Pete actually expended some effort the next morning keeping his mitts off the phone and his ears peeled, but as the hours of the morning skated away empty, he began to gather excuses for her and then, finally, for himself, for being so idiotic as to sit around and wait. He snatched up the phone and dialed.

"Is this Harold Stern?" asked Pete.

"Yeah," said the voice on the phone. "Who wants to know?"

"Peter Bartholomew," said Pete. "I work for a company on Cape Hook called Factotum." The lie was coming easier. "I'm researching a family history and I'm trying to locate a particular Harold Stern who was stationed at the Bradford Air Force Base here on the Hook and later served in Korea during the war. That wouldn't be you, by any chance?"

"No," he said, and he hung up the phone.

Pete dialed the H. Stern who had not answered before. He still didn't answer. He called the home at which the child had answered and got Mrs. Stern this time. Mr. Stern was twenty-eight years old, and his father's name was Paul. He had no uncles, or older cousins, or anyone in the family by the name of Harold. He had no relatives who had served in the Air Force, and to the best of his knowledge he knew no one who had ever been to Cape Hook.

Pete tried the no-answer one more time and got the same result. He stared at the phone for a minute, then picked it up again and dialed Hardy Rogers. Hardy was at the hospital in Bradford. Pete then called Will McOwat. Willy was in, and he agreed to remain in long enough for Pete to get over there to talk to him about the Hitchcocks. It *was* about the Hitchcocks, Pete reassured himself, and it wasn't his fault if the chief was going to assume it was about one particular one.

Having now called everyone it was possible for him to call, with the one exception of Martha, Pete stepped out into the hall to look for Rita.

"Where are the twins?"

"Don't call them 'the twins'—their mother doesn't like it."

Pete looked at Rita. What was he doing to everybody that they were all getting mad at him? "Where," he asked, with most of his cool, "are Bentley and Carlisle?"

Rita examined the ceiling. "Let's see. I sent Carlisle to do Mrs. Hart's shopping. Bentley went with Bill to work on the radio thing. I, in case you're interested, will be here until one P.M., answering the phone and attempting to find the newspaper article Mary Peletier has been asking

171

for, for weeks." She waved at a pile of newspapers on Pete's couch.

Pete had considered asking Rita or one of the twins if they could give a call now and then to the one remaining H. Stern he had been unable to contact, but he now thought better of it. "And what happens at one?" he asked Rita. "Don't suppose you'd opt for lunch with your old partner?"

At once whatever had been bugging Rita flew off. She smiled at him, and the little crow's feet at the corners of her eyes that had grown there from much of this same kind of smiling winked. "I have a date," she said. "Tomorrow?"

Tomorrow was Saturday, the Fourth, and Pete had hoped to make a day of it with Martha, topping it off with dinner at the Whiteaker Hotel. "Let's see what we can work out," he said. "I'm off to the station to meet the chief. Talk to you later."

Dating, it seemed, was beginning to spring out all over.

Will McOwat looked at the two letters in front of him on the table. Pete had carefully folded under the "Love, Mother" sign-off on the one, and he now asked Willy if he thought they could have been written by the same person, almost twenty years apart.

"Could be," said Willy. "Same ys. Same slant."

Pete unfolded the "Love, Mother" letter. "And it's two different people. Or at least it's supposed to be."

Willy looked up at Pete and snapped, "So what's the big point here? I've got things to do!"

Maybe it's the full moon, Pete thought. He was fast running out of pleasant comebacks. And he was worried—very worried—about Martha. He explained what Martha had suggested to Willy, and Willy didn't like it one bit.

"So I wondered if you could get it checked out by a handwriting analyst, just to be sure. I've been thinking a lot about it. Suppose Edna did do something to Lizzie, and someone out there knows about it—or just found out about it—and got back at Edna the same way. It seems a strong coincidence: two sisters, similar deaths; and there must be some reason why Edna was killed."

"We have plenty of reasons," said Willy. "You just don't want to apply them to the person to whom they apply. Do you?"

Pete avoided answering in the way he saw most fit. Willy was still studying the letters, and Pete decided that he wouldn't still be studying them if he wasn't contemplating doing something about them, and therefore he decided to change the subject.

"Found out anything new?"

Willy picked up the letters, returned them to their envelope, and placed them in his shirt pocket.

"Found out anything new." His voice was unnecessarily loud, Pete noticed. "I've found a doctor who makes house calls for no reason on people who are no longer his patients, and I'm the one who's crazy because I think it's strange. I found a woman who suddenly remembers cars on Shore Road on the day of a murder, and after exhaustive questioning, I am able to pin her down to the one fact that the smaller car is not a Ford Escort. I leave with a woman in tears, a husband in a rage, and an unhealthy attitude about one of the two men on my force and a reopened accident

173

case that happened last fall. I spend an entire morning on the phone with the registry and discover that someone upon whose help I had assumed I could count has an ex-wife driving around visiting people the night before they die and then disappearing herself. I've found the entire city of Boston has no idea what happens to its garbage, and I find that another accidental-death case over twenty years old is now being thrown back in my face because *some people assume I have nothing else to do!*"

The phone rang. "What!" he hollered into it, and the rich red that had suffused his face now became an intense purple. "When? Where? Get your ass over there!"

Something about the way he said it made Pete hope he wasn't going to show up for basketball for some time. Pete considered sticking around long enough to explain to him about Hardy, about the island, about how it wasn't that strange for its only doctor to do a few things for some people he'd known most of his life. Pete looked at Willy's still-suffused face once more and decided to leave while he was still able to do so under his own steam.

Connie Bartholomew opened the door of Sarah's house to see a pale and cool-eyed Martha Hitchcock on the step.

"Hello," said Martha.

"Hello," said Connie.

"Hello, Mrs. Abrew," Martha said, and Connie turned around to see Sarah behind her, leaning on her cane and blinking at Martha, the knobby hand on the cane giving off a steady shake. Connie wished she would sit down. She turned back to Martha.

"I would like to speak with you in regard to a personal matter," Martha said, sounding as if she hated her guts, sounding as if she wouldn't be here at all if she could have figured her way around it.

What the hell is this? thought Connie. But she turned behind her and said, "Back in a minute, Sarah," and she practically walked right through Martha as she led the way out the door. No sense in putting things off, she always said.

They walked down the gravel road away from Main Street, and Connie noticed that Martha's stride had to reach to keep up. Connie slowed her steps, and Martha began to talk faster than they were walking.

"I've been told by the police that you were at my mother's house the night before she died, and I would like to know why."

Connie stopped walking. "The police?"

"The police. They haven't found you?"

The cool green eyes stared at Connie.

"*Found* me?"

"They went to the Whiteaker looking for you, but you were gone. You knew my mother?" She waited, and Connie had the distinct impression that there was more to this question than met the ear.

Connie set off walking once again. She was barefoot and wearing gym shorts and a T-shirt, and her long legs and roughened soles floated over the gravel as if she were walking in shoes; but once she noticed that Martha's sneakers had to take a hop to catch up, she slowed again.

"I didn't know her any more than anyone else around here," said Connie, and to her surprise it sounded defensive—very defensive. "Pete's sister

Polly . . ." She turned to look at Martha, and it slowed her down even more. "You know Polly?"

Martha shook her head.

"Polly lives in Maine now. This place got to her, too. . . . Anyway, Polly takes the *Islander.* You get the *Islander?*"

Martha shook her head again. The *Islander* was Nashtoba's newspaper, of sorts, and Connie had never been able to stand it. First you did it and it appeared in the *Islander,* then everybody talked about it, and then what everybody *said* about it appeared in the *Islander.*

"Polly called me, and we got to talking. She told me that your mother's house was advertised for rent, and we got to talking about that; nothing to it, really—just about the house and all. It was always . . ." Connie stopped and gave thought to the idea that Martha might not be too comfortable with the things Connie had been about to say about the house. "That was that. We hung up, and I got to thinking and kind of . . ." Martha was behind again, and Connie was getting tired of the knife-in-the-back feel to the eyes behind her. With an abruptness that left Martha two feet in front of her, Connie stopped and sat down crosslegged in the grass. "Can we stop?"

Martha tucked her denim skirt around her and sat.

Silence. Connie looked at Martha and wished she were still walking after all: The eyes dead-on weren't a whole lot better. But what the hell was she afraid of? That Martha was going to arrest her? Connie looked hard at Martha. They were within the vicinity of a similar age—there couldn't have been more than a year or two between them on

176

whatever side—and Connie couldn't quite figure why she was getting so defensive, as if she were talking to her mother. Connie finally gave a sheepish grin and resumed talking. "I got to missing this obnoxious old place. I called your mother and set up this plan to come see her and talk about the house. That's it."

Martha looked at the grass and began to pull it up, one blade at a time. "You agreed to rent the house?"

Connie decided to solve this eye problem by flopping onto her back and folding her hands behind her head. "Yeah, pretty much. I couldn't pin her down on it, though; she got a little off-track." *Drunk* was the word she was really looking for here, and Connie was somewhat proud of her tact. "So what I did was, I suggested we talk details in the morning." Another pause, this one awkward enough for Connie to guess that Martha had guessed that Connie had returned there the next morning to pump her mother full of pills and dump her in the tub. Was that what this was all about? Connie bolted straight up. "I told her I'd call her in the morning. I figured in the morning . . ." she'd be sober. Connie didn't say it, but somehow she felt, again, that Martha was reading her thoughts, and an unusual wave of pity swept her. "But I didn't call her in the morning because something else got in the way. When I did call, it was about three o'clock, and there was no answer at all. Obviously."

Obviously.

Connie stopped talking. When she stopped talking she stopped: She shut her mouth and looked at Martha and waited for Martha to say something.

She was slightly shocked to see the look that came into Martha's eye, a look that told Connie Martha wanted to belt her.

"If I were you I'd get my ass down to the police station," Martha said as she stood up. "I told them you were at the Whiteaker, but it was some-one else who saw your car at my mother's, not me. But I'm warning you right now, if they ask me I'll tell them you're here. If it's any consolation to you, your husband has been doing his damned-est to keep them off your back." She turned and set off into the road, but then she stopped and looked back at Connie. "And by the way," she added. "When you talk to the cops, don't worry about telling them all the rotten stuff my mother said about me. They already know." She smiled. "And just for the record, so do I."

It was strange. Normally Connie would be screaming after her "Bitch!" or something equally as charming as that. Here Martha had dragged her out of her perfectly comfortable (albeit temporary) home and then had the nerve to act as if she were doing her some favor! But somehow all Connie could do was feel sorry for her. Sorry for her. Connie Bartholomew, whose main motto was fix it or put up with it, was feeling sorry for someone, someone whom she didn't even like. And in a flash, Connie saw exactly what was going to or had already happened: Pete, the world's biggest sucker, was already feeling sorry for her too, and he was going to fall for her hook, line, and sinker.

Connie shrugged off these nauseating thoughts and started back down the road to Sarah's.

*   *   *

Sarah was sitting in her chair again and staring into the air in front of her. "I have to go out, Sarah," Connie said.

"Where?"

Connie didn't believe in humoring people, especially not old people. They needed to have all the facts and use their brains as much as or more than the rest of us did. "I have to go see a cop," said Connie. "It seems I have vital evidence in this famous Hitchcock case. Shouldn't take me long, and it's nothing they can arrest me over. I'll be back for lunch."

She patted Sarah's hand where it still rested clutching the cane, then looked at her more closely. "Sarah?"

"Yes," said Sarah. "Fine." Even for Sarah, it was a little too succinct.

I'll have a long talk with her when I get back, thought Connie, but she was in a hurry. She hopped into her car, put down the top, and headed for the station.

The police chief was new since Connie's day. The minute Connie saw him, her eyes widened in appreciation. Connie was a big woman, but this was the type of man that a big woman could sit on without squashing. She was not four seconds in his presence, however, when her admiration began to fade.

Connie had grown up in a household in which her father set the mood: He could wake up dancing, and in half an hour his gloom could descend and pervade every corner and every person in its black despair. Connie had always since been quick to lose patience with moody people. She felt if you couldn't fake a certain pleasantness, then you should stay home and listen to Joni Mitchell records until it passed. Add to that inbred attitude a certain uneasiness of her own over the events of the morning, and it was surprising that they lasted the whole four seconds before the blow.

"My name is Connie Bartholomew," she said, and instead of thanking her for coming, the chief actually threw a balled-up piece of paper at a plant that was hanging not far from her head.

"Constance B. Bartholomew," he said, and Connie decided that once and for all it was time she did something about that name.

"I hear you were looking for me. I was at Edna Hitchcock's the night before she—"

"Right," said the chief. "And why tell *me* about it? What could *I* possibly want to know for? Just because you might well have been the last person to see her alive—or should I say, second-to-the-last person? Or *should* I say, last person? How about it? I suppose you have some cast-iron—"

Connie walked up to the table and leaned down over the top of the chief's balding head. "Get stuffed," she said.

The funny thing—the really aggravating thing—was that he didn't do anything after she said that. He sat there and looked up at her and started to grin like a fat, full cat.

Chapter
19

Roberta Ballantine reminded Pete very much of her father, and it surprised him very much to see the same friendly and open smile on the face of the woman who had previously hung up on him. The reason for the change Pete took to be his own opening arguments: He was here to talk not to the Hitchcock family lawyer but to the old personal friend of Lizzie Denault. The real reason for the change, he soon found out, was something else.

"So Dad says you think Lizzie had a baby. If she did, it's news to me. Not that it would be impossible, mind you: They were here summers and away long enough; it wouldn't have been hard for her to hide it, not hard at all. Do you know who the father was?"

Pete wasn't here to give out information but to get it. "I would be interested in your own thoughts on—"

"Well!" Roberta Ballantine looked at her watch, pushed a stray forelock of salt-and-pepper hair out of her eyes, and seemed to give about five seconds of thought as to how best to satisfy Pete and then get on with her own program. "Lizzie got all the boys. Edna and I, we were too shy. Edna especially, if I do say so myself; she was very . . . hard to get to know. Very formal. Stiff. Lizzie was . . . different. I was somewhere in between, of course. But Lizzie didn't tell me anything; we weren't like that. Come to that, neither were Edna and I. Edna kept her own counsel. I, on the other hand, used to tell her a few things." A spark that Pete had seen in her father's eye twinkled now in hers. *"My* secrets are of no interest to you though, now are they?" But she seemed to feel that, having implied complete openness if they *were* of interest to him, he would therefore be completely open with her. "So! That's it! The extent of my involvement in the affairs of the Denault girls. Now, what have you gleaned about poor Lizzie's sordid past, other than this suicide?"

Pete looked at Roberta Ballantine and somehow started to doubt that she was really all that open and friendly. She was smart, he decided; but that wasn't going to help him a whole lot, and he had a sneaking suspicion that if he stuck around here much longer she would have wormed some things out of *him* that were not in Martha's best interest to be told. What exactly that could be he didn't know, but he was feeling outmaneuvered and suddenly and peculiarly nervous. He looked upside down and sideways at her watch and said, "Wow!" Back into his Hardy boys mode. "It's late. I've gotta go." And without further discussion, he did. The question he kept asking himself as he drove back to Factotum was whether she was really trying to find out something specific, or if her curiosity fell more accurately under the category of plain old gossip.

Back at Factotum, Pete watched Bill Freed wander past his door without looking in, one of the twins trailing worshipfully behind him, and frowned. There *was* something definitely off-kilter about Bill these days. Pete sat with his hand on the phone and thought about Bill for a minute. Was it something Pete had done? He hadn't seen much of Bill, hadn't had a good talk with him lately; and maybe Rita was right: Maybe it was time he did. They were better friends than they were acting these past few months, and Pete could review this period of time and see that, although it wasn't all his fault, some of it sure was. It was amazing how one's own problems could sap one's strength for dealing with someone else's. And what were his choices? He could go crawling and call Martha, as he had been preparing to do; or he could go out and ask Rita, for the tenth time, if it were possible she had missed any of his calls.

Pete got up from the lawn chair in which he was sitting, pushed past an Igloo cooler and a bird feeder, and walked into the hall. Bill was sitting in what had once been the cottage dining room, at what had once been the dining-room table but was now another Factotum file cabinet: It was piled high with manila folders, old *National Geographic*s, and about two weeks' worth of newspapers.

"Drink?" asked Pete, and Bill jumped up, not bothering to push himself back from the table first, so that he jammed his thighs into it and sent the folders as well as a good week's worth of newspapers cascading to the floor. Pete bent down and came near to having his head cracked by Bill, so

Pete straightened up fast and left Bill to scrabble around and pick up the papers alone. Bill's face was fire-engine red—Pete had never seen anything so red, or maybe it was just the brilliant blueness of his eyes that made his face seem so red—but Pete took the papers out of his hands and began to restack them on the table, and eventually Bill's face had subsided to a dull peach.

"I could use a drink, Bill. How about you?"

Bill seemed to be looking all over the place for something that wasn't Pete's face. "Now?"

"Whenever you say."

Bill pushed back his chair so hard it crashed into the wall behind him. "Yes," he said. "I mean, now. I mean, yes, I will. A drink. I'll drive."

Pete would have argued—Bill's driving was not a big improvement over Bill's walking or Bill's standing or Bill's doorway navigation—but there seemed to be something more noble in the gesture than was immediately apparent, and Pete decided to respect the offer.

"Okay," he said. They stopped to talk to Rita on the way out, but talking to Rita these days was kind of like listening to Ethel Merman: A little of it went a long way. Pete's ears began to singe, and in fifteen minutes they were seated at the bar in Lupo's, looking down into two frosted mugs of Bud.

"I may as well tell you," said Bill, "that I was looking at what you'd done so far in Martha's file. But I guess you knew that."

"No," said Pete, surprised. "I didn't."

"Yes, you did," said Bill. "I was looking in her file, but I didn't see anything. I'll put it back."

"There's not much to see," said Pete, staring at Bill. "I'm not exactly burning up the—"

"What do the police think?" asked Bill. His beer was down two-thirds, and Pete took a good dent out of his own in the hopes of landing on the same wavelength sooner that way. What do the police think? About Martha's cousin?

"They think Martha did it, don't they? You've been talking to the chief, haven't you? Isn't that what they think?"

Pete sighed, remembering Willy. "Yes, I suppose they do."

Bill ordered two more beers. Pete looked at Bill's large frame and remembered the fat-beer-fat theory and tried to relax. Pete was only a couple of years older than Bill; he wasn't Bill's father. He certainly wasn't Bill's keeper. But Bill's bulk wasn't fat, Bill's bulk was all muscle; and Pete wasn't sure that there was a muscle-beer-muscle theory as well.

"Well, this is what I think," said Bill, and out spilled some garbled scenario involving burglars who never got around to burgling, vandals who arrived after the fact to dump dead bodies in tubs for a lark, personal vendettas of old boyfriends as yet to be discovered, and something about the effects of salt air on a person's high blood pressure. The two beers were emptied, and Bill ordered another beer for Pete and a daiquiri for himself.

A daiquiri?

"She keeps telling me I don't love her," said Bill, once he had attacked the new drink, "but I'd like to know what else to call it."

"Who?"

Bill ignored him. "As if she would know! I don't think she ever loved anyone in her life. Really, I mean that: I don't think she has. Oh, I was sure she loved me for a while there—I was sure of it! She was so . . . nice to me. God!" The rest of the daiquiri disappeared.

"Who?" asked Pete again.

Bill ordered another daiquiri, looked at Pete's full beer with surprise, took a sip, and winced. The drinks were beginning to make Pete nervous, for several reasons. Daiquiris? Bill? Pete looked at his watch: It was six-thirty.

"I went crazy over her," said Bill. "It's as simple as that: I think I went out of my mind. The things I did! The lies I told! All those weekends in Boston . . ."

Pete picked up his beer and gulped three times. "Bill," he said quietly, "who?"

Bill whipped his stool halfway around and cracked it into the side of Pete's knee. "I don't know why I did it," he said. "I just don't know why. It was very wrong. I've never done anything so wrong, and while I was doing it nothing ever seemed so right. I thought I was helping her. Saving her! Me!"

Two daiquiris sat in front of them now. Full. Somehow Pete didn't feel the need to ask "who" any more. He looked into the seafoam-green liquid and asked, each word clear and carefully placed, "Did Adrienne find out? Is that what happened?"

"I left her. Martha knew about her from the first. She didn't care. I cared, though, and I left her; and the minute I left Adrienne—almost the very minute—Martha told me there was someone else! What a fool I made of myself! What a fool I still am! I wouldn't take it. I just wouldn't take no. I made a real jerk out of myself when she told me there was someone else." Bill laughed. "Of course there was someone else. What did I think? She'd been sitting around reading romance novels waiting for me to show? Someone like her?" Bill's hand shot out and his drink tipped over. Since the bartender was there with the rag anyway, Bill ordered two more; but since Pete's was still in front of him, that made the count uneven: Bill ordered an extra. The bartender looked at Pete, but Pete couldn't quite figure out why. He sipped out of his two drinks in turn and tried to stop listening to Bill. A large hand gripped Pete's shoulder and held on.

"Pete," said Bill. "Pete. You can't imagine in a million years what a jerk I've been. When I tell you . . ."

"You should have told me," said Pete. If only he had told him.

Bill looked at him. "I should have. I should have. I didn't want to, though; I was afraid to. I didn't know what you'd—"

"For God's sake!" said Pete. "Everyone cheats."

Bill stared at him. "Cheats? Cheats. Yes. Cheats. I didn't want to tell you about that, either; not after what happened with Connie."

Pete pushed back his stool and got up. Someone else. He went to the men's room, and when he came back the bartender and Bill were arguing. Perfect. The perfect ending to a perfect night. "Come on," he said. They clambered into Bill's car and headed off for Knackie's: The fishermen hung out in Knackie's, and no one ever got shut off there—ever. Pete looked at the clock as he walked in and noticed that it was seven-thirty.

The next time Pete looked at the clock it was ten; Bill was arguing with the bartender again, and this time Pete joined in. How is this happening? he asked himself. What happened to the old Pete, the moderate Pete, the sensible Pete, the man who never drank to excess, who never drove if he did, who certainly never got into a car with someone else who did, especially when it was someone who couldn't drive anyway? About a thousand daiquiris, that's what happened to him. Pete was actually attempting to climb over the bar when the proverbial hush descended, and Willy McOwat walked into the room.

It ended peacefully enough. Bill's Rabbit stayed at Knackie's overnight, and Bill and Pete rode home in the back of the Scout. The chief escorted Bill into the Whiteaker and up to his room, and then he drove Pete back to Factotum.

"So what's all this?" he asked Pete, not unnicely, once they were safe in the middle of Pete's kitchen.

"You always pick up the drunks?" asked Pete, not nicely at all.

Willy ran a large glass of water and handed it to Pete. "Not all of 'em. Was a bit surprised when they said it was you, that's all. Your friend do this a lot?"

"Never," said Pete. "Only when love is lost. I thought you were supposed to boil up black coffee."

"Old wives' tale. Drink the water. Hangovers are just dehydration of the brain."

Dehydration of the brain. Pete tossed off the water.

"Anyone I know?" asked Willy.

Pete laughed. "Someone you are intimate with yourself," he said. At least that was what he hoped he said. "You'd think she was the only woman on the island. Martha."

The chief's eyebrows went up. "And your excuse?"

Pete got himself another glass of water. He liked this theory, dehydration of the brain. "Same excuse. Same woman. Only not quite so big a fool. I don't think." Pete stopped and looked at the chief and frowned, trying to remember what he had said to Martha of a personal nature.

"Your friend was seeing her?"

"And seeing her and seeing her. In Boston, even. Here, even. How that one got past the rumor mill would be fun to find out. Must be the same way a guy that big can walk around this place without anyone seeing him. Strange."

"We looked into the handwriting thing," said Willy. "We're not changing our first story."

Pete didn't know what he was talking about, but neither did he care, so he said, "Oh."

"This friend of yours is no longer seeing Martha?"

"No," said Pete. "There's someone else."

Pete narrowed his eyes at the chief. He looked less fuzzy but no less fat. "I was only kidding when I said you were intimate with her, wasn't I?"

"You were. Are *you* still seeing her?"

"It's funny about her," said Pete. He looked up at the ceiling and found it was spinning. He looked down. *"Something* is there. Or something isn't there. Something you keep waiting for, something you think only you are going to get to be in on. Nobody else." Pete barked out a laugh. "Or everybody else."

"You're still seeing her?"

"Not any more," said Pete, in his best Peter Sellers.

"Good," said Willy.

Pete didn't like the sound of that, and a long time after the chief had left, he still didn't like the sound of it.

Connie got up early on the Fourth of July, deciding to take a swim before the parade closed off Main Street and locked her in at Sarah's. She turned onto Main from Sarah's gravel road, and from Main she turned onto Shore and from Shore she turned off past Factotum and on toward the marsh. Pete's truck was at Factotum. She stopped, made a U-turn, and headed the other way, not wishing to run into Pete if he happened, also, to be swimming at the beach by the marsh. She had tried to call him, after thinking over what Martha had said the day before, and had been given an obvious dodge by Rita. The hell with him. She'd swim at the Point. Of course, he could be swimming at the Point just as easily as he could be swimming at the marsh, after all; and she knew that just as when she'd been trying to find him and couldn't, now that she didn't want to find him she would. She drove aimlessly along Shore Road, feeling uncharacteristically indecisive, and found herself driving past the Hitchcock house. She should have said some other things to Martha, should have asked if the house was still for rent, but did she really want to stay here, to find a job, to settle back in to . . . to what? To hiding from Pete? No, she didn't. And if she knew anything about Sarah, Sarah was about one more food-shopping trip away from booting Connie out. She didn't need her there—not really—and now that Sarah had realized that Pete was as stubborn as she was and wouldn't be setting foot there until Connie was gone . . . Connie pulled back into Sarah's road, and as she neared the house she could see a car parked out in front. Hardy Rogers. Connie hit the grass at a gallop.

It was like something out of those 1940s movies she and Pete used to watch on rainy Sundays. Sarah lay propped in her chair, and Hardy was just closing his bag. Connie expected him to say "She's had a bad shock, but she'll be all right. I've given her something to help her sleep."

"*I* don't know what the hell is wrong with you," said Hardy. "Your heart's nice and strong and even. Your blood pressure is fine. If you're feeling anxious—"

"Anxious!" snapped Sarah. "You'd be anxious too if you started seeing spots. I'm all right now, I told you; now be off with you."

Hardy looked at Connie with some speculation in his blue eyes. "You're staying here?"

"Yes," said Connie.

"For a while," said Sarah.

"Well, come by the office next week for a once-over, Sarah, when you're feeling better."

"When I'm feeling better, who needs you?" said Sarah, but Connie had the feeling that she only said it once Hardy had moved far enough off so he couldn't hear.

Connie continued walking with Hardy toward the door. "Thank you." She held out her hand to him, noticed it was shaking, and took it back fast. "Is she really all right?"

Hardy snorted. "Don't ask me. If she doesn't come in next week I'll come back out, but try to get her to make an appointment."

"Thank you," said Connie again.

She returned to the living room.

"Where's Pete?" asked Sarah.

Connie stared at her. "I have no idea where Pete is."

"I tried to call him, and Rita Peck gave me a song and a dance. I want to talk to him."

"Well, I can't pull him out of my hat, Sarah." Connie didn't mention seeing his truck.

Sarah glared at her. "Well, go find him, will you?"

Connie narrowed her eyes at Sarah. "Are you sure you're all right?" She didn't look exactly right, but Connie suspected that much of this was another get-Connie-and-Pete-together ploy.

The cane snapped onto the floor. "Of course I'm all right! I want to talk to him, that's all. Are you going to go find him or not?"

And now she did look all right, more like the old Sarah, and that decided it for Connie. "Not," she said.

Sarah glared at her some more. "Then sit down and shut up if I'm going to have to talk to *you*."

* * *

There was a knock on the door that Pete chose to ignore. Whoever was knocking chose to ignore his ignoring of it: He heard it open, heard the click of heels on his kitchen floor; he opened one eye and saw Rita standing in his doorway.

"It's nine o'clock, Pete, and Bill is waiting for you to pick him up so he can go get his car. He's on the phone. Do you want me to tell him . . ."

Pete sat up. His stomach rose with him and then kept on rising up into the middle of his chest. He realized he was naked, and he carefully balled up the sheet in his lap.

"Apparently you told him last night you would pick him up at eight-thirty this morning at the hotel. Do you want me to tell him—" Rita's eyes widened and narrowed as Pete gave a muffled burp.

"I'll be right there. Would you mind telling him I'll be right there? I'm sorry." Pete tried to look blamefully at his alarm clock.

"What's the *matter* with you?"

"Dehydration of the brain," said Pete, and he would have tried to say something more, but he could feel another burp rising. He gave up.

"And Sarah called several times. She wanted to talk to you, and she said it was important, and she wants you to call her right back."

"Well, I can't now, can I?" Pete stood up, his top sheet carefully draped around his waist, and moved toward the bathroom.

"She's already called twice, and it's only nine o'clock."

"I know what it's about, and I'm not falling for it. Tell her we're at war with Russia. Tell her she's about to be sent to the Front."

"I'll be happy to call her back for you and tell her you don't wish to speak with her." It was Rita's best "up to you" voice, and Pete didn't fall for that, either.

"Good," he said from the bathroom, where he was looking at his alien face in the mirror.

"And Connie called. She asked if you could call her at Sarah's. I told her I wasn't sure when I'd be seeing you next."

Pete couldn't think of anything to say to that one. He heard heels click across the floor—away from him this time.

"And since I *still* don't know when I'll be seeing you next, unless it's tonight at the Whiteaker for dinner . . ."

Tonight. Dinner. John Clark's dinner. And Martha. Martha, who was just about the only person who had *not* called; and after the revelations of last night, Pete could see why she hadn't. Bill Freed. And someone else. He took three fast strides out of the bathroom and stopped to wait for his stomach to catch up. "Rita!" he hollered. "I can't come to dinner! Will you tell John, please, and thank him, but I'm sorry."

They looked at each other down the length of the kitchen.

"You dislike him that much?" asked Rita softly, and Pete wasn't sure, but it seemed from afar that her eyes were getting bright.

"No," said Pete, "it's not that . . ."

But Rita was gone. The old Pete would have chased her out into the office in his bedsheet. The new Pete turned around and spent too long in the shower, and when he did go back out he walked past Rita without stopping, despite the fact that she was on the phone, fighting, again, with Maxine.

Bill's plum-colored VW Rabbit was not alone when he and Bill pulled up into the back of Knackie's to collect it. Will McOwat was leaning against the driver's door, and Paul Roose was on his hands and knees, almost under one of the tires, testing the lug nuts.

"I thought you guys said eight-thirty," said Willy, looking at his watch. "Not that I have anything else to do now."

Bill Freed had stopped in his tracks, and somehow Pete didn't think it was anything to do with letting his stomach catch up to him; up until now, Bill had seemed to be in pretty good shape.

"What's going on?" asked Pete.

"Is this your car, Mr. Freed?" Willy asked Bill. Bill nodded.

Willy straightened up. "Then I would appreciate a word with you back at the station." He looked at Pete. "In private."

Bill looked at Pete, and Pete looked at Bill.

"What . . ." began Pete, but then he looked at Willy and experienced a certain *déjà vu.* "I'll leave," he said instead.

"No," said Bill. "There's no need for you to go. You can say whatever you have to here, Chief."

"Up to you," said Willy, sounding very much like Rita, but when he next spoke he didn't sound much like Rita at all. "Could you tell me, please, what you were doing at Edna Hitchcock's house on June 15?"

* * *

Connie took her feet off the coffee table, sat up, and looked at Sarah. She had known it, somehow, had known all along that there was more to Sarah's state of mind than just failed attempts at rematching Connie with Pete.

"Why didn't you tell Pete this before?" Connie asked her. "You knew he was looking so hard for just this kind of information."

"He won't come here, it's his own fault. *You* tell him."

Connie looked down again at the letter that Sarah had thrust into her hands. Why does everyone save letters? Connie wondered. She always threw hers out, and she felt it was only common courtesy that others did the same with hers. She didn't want some hasty words scrawled on paper coming back to haunt her—what, some thirty-odd years later. She shook her head and read the letter again.

Dear Sarah,

I'm in trouble, and I need someone to talk to, and you know what Mother is like. Edna says it would kill Mother, but I'm starting to think she's just as bad. I don't know what to do, and Edna's got it all planned, and I just don't know what's right and I need you to tell me like you always do. I'm pregnant. And Hal's shipped out. I wrote, and he called, and he was miserable about it, but he said we should get married and he sounded like he meant it, but Edna says he's just saying it because he has to, and she says it will never work out. She thinks I should go away, but I keep think-

ing maybe she's wrong and I should wait for
Hal and not give this baby up. Please help me.
                                    Love, Lizzie

"You say Pete didn't call you back, either?"
Connie shook her head. "Did you answer Lizzie's letter?"
"Of course I did. Then you'll have to go get
Pete yourself."
Connie looked down at the rug and counted to
ten. Sarah seemed to be able to read her mind; at
nine and a half she spoke up.
"All right, all right. Let me tell you about it,
and then you can get him to listen. Hush up now
and let me talk."
As if Connie hadn't been trying for an hour now
to get her to do just that. It might have been her
imagination, but it seemed to Connie that Sarah
swayed a bit in her chair. She leaned forward—the
better to hear her, the better to catch her, or the
better to strangle her, she hadn't quite decided
which.
"All right. I answered the letter. We'd gotten
pretty close, Lizzie and I; I made clothes for them
and they used to come over to get fit after school,
and then Mary would pick them up later. Edna fell
off after a while, but Lizzie used to keep coming
just to visit—she liked it here." The implication
was that Lizzie knew something wonderful that
Connie obviously did not. "Edna and her mother
were quite alike, but Lizzie, she was different, not
getting along all that well with the thinking at
home, and over the years she took to asking my
advice, and I took to giving it. It was all right at
first—things like should she tell the teacher it was

Ellen Burns who stole the chalk; things like that. Then it got to be bigger troubles, and for a while she wouldn't come back here when I told her to stop sneaking up the beach after dark; and then when it was too late she decides to make it up and sends me this letter, crying for help." Sarah stopped talking.

"So you answered the letter?"

Sarah looked down at her hands. "I told her to do what Edna said. A flighty eighteen-year-old like Lizzie was no one to be raising a family; I told her that."

"She did what you said?"

Sarah looked up at Connie and away. She blinked. "Yes. She did what I said."

So that was that. Connie put the letter down on the coffee table. "So she gave the baby up. I don't suppose you were included on the hows and wheres?"

When Sarah began to speak again, it was very softly, and Connie was not sure that she was supposed to hear.

"I never imagined it would turn out the way it did. Nobody did. Not Arthur, not Mary; I don't think even Edna herself ever once imagined it. Lizzie couldn't do it, you see. She had that baby; somewhere off in upstate New York they went, Edna and Lizzie together, and Frank back and forth from Boston now and then. The baby was born, and some damned fool let Lizzie hold her, and that was that."

Connie looked up. "What do you mean? She never kept it. . . ."

Sarah sighed. The hand on the cane, Connie noticed, had started to tremble. "She wanted to.

They all tried to talk some sense into her, but she wouldn't listen. She wasn't about to let that child out of her life, and that was that. They called me, I tried to reason with her, she wouldn't listen; that's when Edna came up with her big idea.'' Sarah took a small white handkerchief out of her shirtsleeve and blew her nose. "She and Frank had been married a couple of years by then, but they had no children of their own; I didn't give it much thought at the time; assumed they would sooner or later—Edna was the type who always did what was expected.'' Sarah looked up from where she was carefully folding the handkerchief and peered at Connie. "And there's no need to give a look like that, young lady; there's nothing wrong with doing what's expected. There's a lot worse things you could do than what's expected.''

Connie did not need to ask what, exactly, in her own life was not living up to Sarah's expectations. She attempted to get the train back on the track. "So what did Edna come up with, Sarah? What was her big idea?''

Sarah seemed to be having trouble, all of a sudden, with her throat. She set to coughing. Connie waited. She wondered, while she waited, where Pete was now, but it wasn't something she would have wondered if she'd had anything better to do.

"Lizzie was insisting she wasn't going to let the child go, and Mary and Arthur—and Edna, of course—were terrified she'd just traipse on home with the baby in a basket as open and airy as you'd please. So Edna decided to take it.''

It took Connie a moment. Then she stood up. "She what?''

"She and Frank took the baby and adopted her

all legal; that way they could all go home with heads held high. Edna had been gone just about as long as Lizzie, see, and no one could have known it wasn't really she who had the baby. Frank was working in Boston and wasn't around much anyway, so it wasn't really so odd that he had made no announcement. He joined them in New York, and they brought Martha home as theirs."

Poor Pete, thought Connie. All this work for nothing, and all this time Sarah had known.

Chapter
20

In the end, all four of them adjourned to the station after all, Bill reiterating his desire for Pete to remain present, and after some discussion, Willy agreed. They were lined up two on a side of a massive wooden table, and Bill was doing his chameleon-on-a-beet trick. Pete looked at Willy and learned something about him he hadn't known before: The chief didn't like it when people were afraid of him, as Bill was now.

"I didn't kill her," said Bill suddenly, and everyone looked up.

"Wait a minute," said Pete. "Aren't we supposed to be telling Bill to talk to a lawyer?"

The chief and Paul Roose were both looking surprised at Bill's outburst, and neither answered.

"I don't need a lawyer," said Bill. "I didn't kill her. I went there after she was dead."

Pete stared at him.

"You went there to do what, Mr. Freed?" asked Willy.

Bill leaned forward. "To talk to her. To fix

things up. To make her understand about Martha. I didn't plan to do it. . . ." Then he half stood up and went completely white. "I *didn't* do it," he corrected himself, to Pete.

Pete stared.

"What time did you arrive at Mrs. Hitchcock's, Mr. Freed?"

Bill spoke fast, eager to answer. "I don't know. Five, six o'clock. I went right from Factotum; maybe Rita will remember when I left. I'd been thinking all day long about the night before in Boston; Martha and her mother had a terrible fight on the phone, and I couldn't believe some of the things she was saying."

Pete winced. "I think a lawyer—"

"Mr. Freed is not being charged with anything, Pete," said Willy. "He's come in of his own accord to explain the presence of his tire tracks in Edna Hitchcock's drive on or about June 15, and that's where it stands right now."

But Pete noticed that where Willy had at first implied knowledge of Bill's presence there on the day Edna died, it was now "on or about"; now, after he knew from Bill's own lips that he had been there on the very day, he was admitting what he had not known before. What else would Bill let loose? Pete didn't have time to wonder whether his concern was for Bill himself or for the daughter who was saying terrible things about her mother the night before her mother was killed. "Bill," said Pete, "I could call Roberta Ballantine for you."

Bill waved him off and kept on. "I tried to talk to Martha, but she was so upset. It was hurting her so badly, I could tell. I wished I could fix it. Martha had fixed things with me, had helped me when my wife and I . . ." He trailed off, and Pete had time to notice how easily some people could say that phrase "my wife and I." Pete had stumbled over it every time he'd tried to use it, objecting to its possessive tone. Had he known, on some subconscious level, how soon his "possession" would end?

"I went to the Point," Bill went on, and then he stopped as Willy interrupted.

"You knew the house? Knew where Edna Hitchcock lived?"

Pete almost smiled. That was The Bean for you: Everyone on Nashtoba knew that house.

"I knew the house," Bill reiterated. He seemed relieved to have someone read him his lines.

"And then what?"

"And then what?" Belatedly, Bill realized he was once again on his own, and he stumbled on, starting slow and getting faster. "I knocked and there was no answer. I was going to walk around the porch to the front in case someone was on the beach, and I walked by the window at the end of the porch and just happened to look in, and there she was, on the floor."

"On the floor?" Willy glared at Pete, as if accusing Pete of lying all along about finding her in the tub, as if Pete would have run the water himself. Pete began to think that Willy was a bit of a jerk.

"Where, exactly, on the floor was she?"

"Right by the couch. As if she tumbled off; her arm was underneath her. It didn't look right. I knocked on the glass and she didn't move. I went back to the door and it wasn't locked, so I went in and . . ." The rush of words came to a dead stop. "I saw she was dead."

Willy rubbed a hand over his forehead, creating puckered lines that remained when he removed his hand. "What else did you see, Mr. Freed?"

Bill looked at Pete. "There were pills there. And a liquor bottle. The pill bottle was empty."

"Did you read the label on the pill bottle?"

Bill's neck became, again, hot pink. "No," he said.

Willy looked at Paul Roose, who was writing quickly. "You saw no drug name on the bottle?"

"No."

"No patient name?"

"No."

"The name of the prescribing doctor?"

"No." Bill's whole face was suffused. He was lying.

Pete closed his eyes.

"Then what did you do, Mr. Freed?"

Bill cleared his throat. "I know this was wrong. I know now it was wrong. At the time . . ." He sat up straighter and looked hard at the two policemen and then at Pete. "At the time it seemed to be the right thing to do. I was afraid . . . I was afraid of how others would look at what I was seeing. I decided to make it look like an accident, like Edna had drunk too much in the tub and gone under. I . . ."

If Pete could for one minute have imagined what Bill was about to say he would have stopped him, but never in his wildest dreams would he have believed one man could be so dumb.

"I removed her clothes and put her in the tub and placed the bottle beside her. I wiped everything off. I washed out the glass. I pressed her hand back around it and back around the bottle.

Then I filled the tub with water." He stopped, tired out, as if he had just now, again, carried that dead weight up the full flight of stairs.

Silence. All three men stared at Bill. Bill looked down.

The chief cleared his throat. "And why, Mr. Freed, did you use hot water?"

Bill raised his head and looked at the chief with eyes that were soft and intensely blue and blank. "Hot water?"

"In the tub, Mr. Freed. The water was hot, steaming hot."

"I always run my bathwater hot," he answered, and Willy stood up suddenly and moved to the window. He was there for a very long time.

Connie sat and looked at Sarah and wondered what it was about this interfering old woman that attracted people to her—people like Lizzie Denault, people like Pete and herself. Why did any of them give the least little damn about what she thought?

"We all thought it would work," said Sarah, with a new defensiveness in her tone. "Lizzie called me, and Mary called me, and I told Lizzie to do it. I told her to sign. She could still see the baby this way, see—she wouldn't lose her completely—but the baby would have a good, safe, normal home, with two caring, responsible parents. We all thought so. All of us." She looked hard at Connie, as if daring her to deny her logic. "Then all of a sudden, Lizzie started to fall apart."

"What . . ."

"There the little thing was, with Edna and Frank—they were living over in the Patterson place then—and there Lizzie was, still living at the Point with Arthur and Mary. Lizzie started to make trouble, wanting the baby with her more, trying to do this, that, and the other, when Edna wanted to do the other, that, and this. Lizzie would come to me crying her eyes out, storming and ranting around here about how hateful they were all being to her, and there was no talking reason to her. Finally she told me she was going to take the baby back.''

Connie, who had been thinking about standing up and heading off to find Pete so he could get over there and hear all this, now settled back down and folded her bare feet up under her on the couch.

"She asked, first. She asked Edna for Martha back. Of course, Edna said no. Then Lizzie started in on old Weiniger.''

"Weiniger?''

"The lawyer who set this all up in the first place, up in Boston; someone Frank lined up for them. Lizzie tried to get him to get Martha back. Things got ugly; Weiniger wasn't about to do anything, but Lizzie threatened to go public with the whole thing, and who knows what would have happened if she hadn't drowned?''

If she hadn't drowned.

Sarah blew her nose again. "Or leastways that's what we all were led to believe at the time. Turns out it was something deliberate—and not surprising, I can tell you now; not one bit surprising. Lizzie was a mess, she couldn't go on the way she was, she . . .'' Sarah leaned forward and looked hard at Connie. "If that baby had been with her all along, you can see it wouldn't have worked out any better, can't you? On the one hand, you have

206

this unstable girl, no husband; and on the other hand you have this nice married couple, two people with their heads on their shoulders, and the fellow with a good career to boot. How was I to know? How was I to know that after Lizzie died it would all go to hell in a handbasket just the same?"

Connie picked up an old newspaper that must have been lying on the coffee table since Pete had last been there. She began to twist it in her hands and the black came off on her fingers, but she didn't care. She opened her mouth to say something, but there wasn't much she could say; and while she was mulling it all over, Sarah wound herself up again.

"Nobody was more surprised than me when Edna started cracking up herself. I tell you, in my day people were built to take their troubles better. I think Martha was about two when it got bad enough so's we all could notice; Edna started popping in on me all of a sudden at all these odd times, making me tell her we'd done the right thing and it wasn't her fault. See what happened?"

"No," said Connie. She didn't. Her ears were tired.

Sarah rapped the floor with her cane. "Of course you do! She dragged that child out of her sister's hands. Because she was the more fit mother, she told herself. Then Edna started worrying that maybe she wasn't the most fit mother after all, that maybe she had made a mistake, that maybe her sister would be alive and Martha would be better off if she had never interfered."

Sarah stopped talking. For some time she stared

down at the hand that rested in her lap, holding the handkerchief.

"I tried to talk to her," she continued, her voice quivering now. "I had never gotten anything going with Edna the way I had with Lizzie. Edna didn't seem to need people the way Lizzie did, somehow, but I tried to talk some sense into her, to get her to face up to her responsibility to the child and go on from there and do the best she could. It was no use. She began seeing Lizzie in the girl. Martha had a certain look about her, always had—that fine, dusty kind of hair; and something about her voice that was kind of deep, like Lizzie's. Every time Martha did something wrong, to Edna it was as if her sister were throwing it all back up in her face. We had one royal send-off fight over it, right here." Sarah pointed with her cane to a spot on her rug that must have haunted her ever since. "I told her to shape up. I slapped her. She never came back." Sarah leaned against the throne back of her chair and closed her eyes. With her eyes closed, Connie began to feel nervous.

She cleared her throat. "What happened to that fellow Hal, the one she mentioned in the letter? Martha's real father?"

Sarah opened her eyes and sighed. "I suppose Edna dished that up onto her plate of guilt as well. How would things have turned out if she'd let Lizzie go on ahead and marry the man?"

There was no mention of Sarah's own portion of guilt, but Connie could almost see it in the air between them like a yellow-brown cloud.

"Didn't he come back? Didn't he try to see Lizzie? Didn't he have anything more to say about it?" Connie was feeling some impatience with the man: How could he let his life walk away from him like that without at least *calling*, for Pete's sake?

Sarah shook her head from side to side. "I don't know. He did, I believe, make some sort of trouble, but Edna dealt with him somehow."

"And why didn't you tell Pete? He's been running around like a nut." Although, thought Connie, from all available signs he hadn't exactly been minding.

Sarah rubbed her hands up under her glasses. "I had to think it through. I wasn't sure what good would be served; who it would help and who it would hurt. I had to think it through. And besides," continued Sarah, looking up with a set to her chin that had previously been missing, "any fool could listen to him talk and see he was going nuts over her, and Martha as messed up as both of the sisters put together. The less he had to do with her the better; the less involved she got to feel with him the better, and him with her. And then *you* came back and I figured it was all . . ."

Connie stared at Sarah. It seemed there weren't going to be any lessons learned here.

Almost at once, Sarah seemed to read that thought also. "And now when I want to come clean over it all and leave people alone to work out their own problems, he won't get near enough for me to let him do it!" She pulled herself up straight and snapped the cane onto the rug with a thump. "So are you going to get out of here and go find him, or do I have to do everything myself?"

Pete was ushered from the room by Paul Roose, as Willy began instructing Bill about calling a lawyer, and behind him Pete could hear Bill going on and on, informing the police how he threw the pill bottle that he found in Edna's living room out of his car window into the white-pine woods by Eldred's. Paul Roose dropped Pete off at Knackie's where his truck remained, not speaking at all on the ride, which was just as well, since Pete never would have heard him.

Once Pete was left alone with his truck, he found himself unable to put his mind to driving it. He walked down the road to a patch of eelgrass and sat down and continued with his thoughts, which were not very reassuring, considering the circumstances. It seemed to Pete that one of two things was now going to happen: Either Willy was not going to believe Bill—and if he didn't believe him it was likely he would charge him with Edna's murder. If he did believe Bill, he would charge him with a felony, anyway, and if he did believe Bill, there was only one reason why he would, and that did not smell like good news for Martha. Why would Bill have gone to all that trouble with the body and the pills? If Edna had appeared dead by her own hand, why had he felt it necessary to alter the evidence? The only answer to that was that she had not appeared to Bill to be dead by her own hand, and the only person whom Bill would have bothered interfering over was Martha; so what was it that had incriminated Martha to Bill? What had he altered? For one thing, he had altered the location of the body; but Pete couldn't find anything too sinister about Martha's mother being in the living room dead, versus being dead in the bath. The hot water? Pete would have laughed about the hot water if he had felt capable of laughing about anything. So what else? The pills. The bottle of pills that had somehow alarmed Bill enough that he threw them in the woods. That, of course, was it. The bottle of pills must have been the same bottle of pills he had seen at home at Martha's, the bottle that had been prescribed by Hardy that Martha had taken with her, not the bottle prescribed by Brixton. Add to that the fact that he had heard the fights between mother and daughter—could well have heard them arguing about the house, the will . . . No. Pete stood up. There was a third possibility, the one they had settled on before the whole hot-water issue came up: Edna had accidentally or on purpose taken too many pills—too many of *Brixton's* pills—and died on the living-room floor, and Bill had come along and for whatever misguided reasons did what he had done. But why would he have done it if he hadn't recognized the bottle of pills? And *how* could he have done it? How could he have carried a dead woman up the stairs, removed her clothes, put her in a bathtub and . . .

Pete began to walk down the road toward his truck. He realized he knew nothing whatsoever about people, or about love, but despite everything he was still sure that Martha was not capable of murder; and if Bill could do all he had done just on the off-chance that she had been involved, the least Pete could do would be to go to the white-pine woods and find that bottle that he was sure would be Brixton's bottle and show it to the chief and say, There!

Chapter
21

Of course, thought Connie, all you have to do around here is think a thing and then it comes true. Now when she wanted to find Pete he was nowhere, and she couldn't even lay eyes on his truck.

She drove by Factotum, but since the truck wasn't there she didn't stop. She had had her daily line of crap from Rita and she knew better than to go looking for another. She drove down Main Street instead, heading for Beston's, pulled up in front, and hollered from her car to the men on the porch.

"Anyone seen Pete?"

The three men exchanged glances with one another, and Connie, with effort, controlled her irritation.

"Nope," Bert hollered. "See the parade?"

The parade! Christ, who needed the parade? "Is he working today, do you know?"

Three pairs of shoulders shrugged. What a bunch of losers.

"They've got Bill Freed down the station," said Evan. "You could try for Pete down there. Picked him up this morning."

Bill Freed at the station? "Thanks," said Connie, and she peeled out into the dust.

Martha packed up her few remaining belongings and stuffed them into the tomato box. Was she always going to be running away from this place? She looked around the boathouse and saw at once that she was going to miss it; she was going to miss Nashtoba, she was going to miss the house, now that it was all over, now that there wasn't a single tie left. It was too bad, really, that there wasn't a way she could work it so that once she was off-island she could call up Connie Bartholomew and see if she still wanted to rent the place. It wasn't Connie's fault, all this—not all of it; it might be Connie's fault that he was the way he was, but it wasn't Connie's fault that Martha was the way *she* was, and Martha had a feeling that Connie truly loved that old house the same way Martha once had.

Martha stood up and shook her head as if to clear it, as if it were an Etch-A-Sketch that she could clean off and start new. Yes, that was what she had done: cleaned it all off so that she could start new. It was over, all of it, dead and buried; it was time to go. The only people who had to worry about any of it now were the police chief and Bill Freed; and Pete, if he were going to be so foolish as to give it another thought. She was sorry when she heard about Bill, but it wasn't her fault— not that part of it—and it wasn't her fault about Pete, either. He'd gotten a thousand dollars and a

good screw, hadn't he? What else did she owe
him? Maybe some day he would actually find her
cousin, and if he did he might find a way to tell
her about it, but she couldn't wait around now to
find out; not now that they had Bill in there, poor,
stupid, blabbermouth Bill.

Martha looked out the window at the harbor and
thought of her mother's house and of the last time
she had been in it with Pete. She left the tomato
box in the middle of the living room, picked up
her car keys, and headed down the steps. She
needed to see it. She needed, at least, to drive by
it one more time.

But as soon as the gray stalking shape came into
view, a crushing lethargy oppressed her. She got
out of her car but passed by the wooden porch
steps and went around to the front and down the
stone steps to the beach. She lay down in the sand
and let the July sun do what four daiquiris and a
long night the night before had not: She slept.

Connie strode into the police station in her bare
feet and walked up to Jean, the dispatcher. There
was no old blue truck outside, but still she decided
to ask. "Is Peter Bartholomew here?"

Jean's eyes popped alive at the sight of Connie.
"Connie! How nice! No, he's left." Her face
pinched up into one of her famous I-know-but-I-
can't-tell-you looks, which told Connie all she
really needed to know: Jean had no idea where he
was.

"Is Bill Freed here?"

Jean nodded. "Talking to Roberta Ballantine."
She willed Connie with her eyes to ask her what
he was talking to Roberta about.

Connie did not ask. She got back into her car and swung out past Lupo's, but Pete's truck wasn't there; and then she turned onto Shore Road with no particular plan in mind and found herself heading out toward the Point. She passed the Secret Place and swung in, but he wasn't there, either. As she drew opposite The Spookhouse, she noticed that Martha Hitchcock's yellow VW was there, but Pete's truck was not. She supposed Martha could have picked him up. . . . And what was she going to barge in on? No, thanks. There was nothing for it but to return to Factotum and leave a message with Rita and forget the whole thing.

It was odd walking into Factotum again, into a place where she, Connie, had once actually lived, seeing again the sagging couch and the 1930s floor-lamp, seeing Rita still perched at her desk and sniffing into the phone. Had she been crying?

"I don't know *where* Pete is," she said. "I *never* know where he is any more. He was supposed to pick up Bill at the hotel and take him to pick up his car *hours* ago."

Yes, something was wrong with Rita. Connie elected not to mention Bill's whereabouts while Rita was in this reduced condition. "Where was Bill's car?" she asked.

"At Knackie's. Something was wrong with him and he said it was dehydration of the brain. What does that *mean?* Honestly, I don't even know what he *means* any more! So how am I supposed to figure out where he is? The one place he was supposed to be he isn't going to be, of course, as if it *mattered*. And I'm not even counting lunch—lunch was indefinite. But dinner wasn't. Dinner was . . . *I* don't care if he doesn't want to eat with us, but

215

you'd think they could at least be a little *polite* about it. John said he didn't care either—we would go anyway, just the three of us; and then Martha called and said she was leaving the island unexpectedly and couldn't come either.''

"Leaving!" said Connie. It figured. It just figured.

Rita looked up at her. She had definitely been crying, and somehow or other it seemed that it was all Pete's fault, which was strange. Pete would never do anything to hurt Rita—at least the old Pete Connie used to know wouldn't.

"That's just what John said. 'Leaving!' Just like that. Like it's a likely story, or something. He didn't say anything else, he didn't say anything about Pete, but I knew he was mad just the same, and I don't blame him. I mean, how rude! And what I'm still doing here, *I* don't know, on the Fourth of July!" She got up from behind her desk and came around to the front. "And in case you think I didn't give him your messages, I did. I've decided it's absolutely ridiculous for two grown people to go around *hiding* from each other all the time.''

Connie had once been used to seeing Rita wound up, but she had never seen her quite like this before. "I'm not hiding, Rita," she said, very quietly, for her. "I'm looking for him, remember? Sarah needs to talk to him, and it's important. It's about this job he's doing for Martha Hitchcock.''

"I *told* you he was going to Knackie's to get Bill's car. That's all I know. I don't even know *him* any more. If I ever on my worst day would have believed he could have talked the way he did about Sarah this morning, or . . .''

216

Or me? wondered Connie.

Connie half-wanted to stay and do something about Rita, but she didn't know what to do. She decided to take one quick swing by Knackie's to look for Pete, and then the hell with it. The hell with all of them.

Pete had walked right past his truck and one hundred feet in the other direction before he realized what he'd done. He stopped, turned one hundred and eighty degrees, reversed himself ninety, and hit the grass on the other side of Knackie's, still thinking.

There was nothing he could do for Bill now. By now Roberta Ballantine would already be there, and she would take care of Bill; but was there something more than looking for that pill bottle that he could be doing for Martha? And did he want to be doing things for Martha? She had told Bill there was someone else. Told Bill. She hadn't really said anything just like that to Pete now, had she? But then again, all Pete had to do was to think about her strange behavior the other night in the boathouse. "I have to meet someone." There was no way he could interpret that as the sign of a relationship that was progressing, could he? But so what? What did his personal involvement have to do with anything? No matter what version of events Will McOwat chose to believe, it was certain he was going to want to talk again to Martha, and didn't Martha deserve to know just how much Bill Freed had said and just how much he hadn't? Should he go find Martha, or butt out? And who do I think I am? Pete asked himself. Why do I think what I do is so important? The police found out about Connie without him, they found out about Bill without him; Martha would find out about Bill without him. But Martha was not the police. Martha was not . . . Martha was . . .

Pete got up and started back to the truck. He was getting sick of it all. He no longer knew who or what anyone was, and they could all act like complete idiots without his help. There was no reason for him to start acting like one too.

Okay, thought Connie, go ahead and explain *that*. Bill's car was still at Knackie's, but then again, so was Pete's truck. Without Pete. Connie got out of her car and climbed into the truck and saw the key in it. Always and forever you will remain a trusting soul, she said to herself. Maybe when he got here the truck hadn't started? She turned the key, and after some low moans it started. So much for that. She turned the truck off again and looked around.

On the floor there were two or three plastic coffee cups and a doughnut bag from Mable's; on the seat were a faded pair of cotton shorts, a new oil filter out of its box, an old newspaper, three pencils, a piece of paper towel on which was written in big letters "BUY RAZOR BLADES," a plastic duck lawn ornament, the crushed oil-filter box, and a baseball glove. On the dash were assorted coins, many chewed and twisted plastic coffee stirrers, and a small rubber Goofy glued to the spot where someone else's St. Christopher statue would be. As she ticked off one by one the still familiar sights and smells of the man she used to love, a rotten gray gloom crept over her, but Connie wasn't one to let the gloom get the upper hand. "The hell with you," she said aloud, and she turned around and looked straight into his brown and troubled eyes.

"Christ!" she hollered. "What the hell are you doing here?"

"Getting my truck," he said.

He waited, frowning.

"Oh," said Connie. "Yes, I'll get out then."

He raised a hand to help her down, then let it fall before actually touching her. He looked away.

As bad as all that, huh?

"Sarah sent me to find you," said Connie. On impulse she slid back across the seat to make room for him behind the wheel, but still he didn't move.

"I have to go," he said. "Bill's been arrested and—"

"Arrested!" Somehow she had never let it enter her head that Bill was at the station, and talking to a lawyer, because of something for which he could actually have been arrested. Either Bill's plight or Connie's face must have snapped Pete out of whatever it was that was holding him there outside the driver's-side door: He climbed up and slid into the seat and began to tell her about Bill.

Rita began to feel a bit edgy around four-thirty, since John had said he'd come by for her at four. They weren't planning to go out until later, of course, but he usually came early and they sat around a bit and talked, and if it was a weekend day like this one, when Maxine was with her father . . . But what she needed mostly today was talk. Why was Pete acting like this? Rita knew it wasn't that he was jealous—not really; not unless she counted the fact that he was probably miffed that she wasn't around as much to wait on his every whim. True, she could tell he didn't much like John, and Rita couldn't understand that: What was there not to like? Even Maxine didn't like him, but Maxine was at that age where she didn't like anybody. Except her father, of course. And Pete. Of course. And to be fair, wasn't the reason she was mad at Pete the very same reason she was attributing to him? Not so much the dinner business—although that really *had* been rude—but the fact that he wasn't around to pick up her own pieces, hold her hand after her fight with Maxine, listen to her own worries and tell her it was all going to be all right. *Lord,* it was confusing sometimes. But really, why was she getting so angry with him this morning? She and Pete usually drove each other crazy once or twice a day, anyway, but this had been different. This morning Pete hadn't been himself at all. So couldn't she give him that— one day of not being himself—without writing the poor guy off? After all, wasn't he there when she needed him *most* of the time?

Rita looked at her watch. And where the heck was John?

"A picture if I ever saw one," said a voice, and Martha opened her eyes and looked up into those of John Clark.

She scrambled to a sitting position and rearranged her denim skirt back to where it belonged. She looked around, saw the sun much lower in the sky, and blinked.

"I fell asleep. What time is it?"

John Clark shot back the cuff of his shirt, which was the palest beige under a light tan suit, and looked at his watch, which was gold. He looked odd, standing on the sand in a frilly pair of loafers in front of her mother's house.

"Almost five. I've been standing here for some time, watching you; I hope you don't mind. By a lucky chance I spotted your car and strolled around this way in the hopes of finding you. I wanted a word."

Martha blinked again. A word. Right. She knew what the word was—with all men it came around to that same word; it would just remain to be seen how clever John Clark would be in getting around to it, how he would rationalize Rita out of the picture and Martha right smack in. At least temporarily. At least for twenty minutes or so.

He made a motion as if to lower the impeccable suit into the sand. "May I? Or could I persuade you to offer me something more conventional in the way of a seat?" He looked back up at the house, and Martha smiled. Not bad, for starters. Then she frowned at the suit. Or had the signals gotten crossed? Did he think she was expecting a ride to the hotel for dinner after all?

"I called Rita," said Martha, as she scrambled to her feet. "Didn't she give you the message? I'm afraid I can't make the dinner this evening; I have to leave. Tonight."

"I was disappointed," said John. "And frankly, that's why I came. I realized that if I didn't catch you today it would be my very last chance."

Cute, thought Martha, but not new. She led him up to her mother's house, pushed open the big wooden door, and tried not to let him see her hesitate inside. Where to take him? The living room was the proper room for guests, of course, but the thought of the Oriental rug made her pause. The dining room had the glasses for the drinks, but then there was the kitchen. She at once thought of Pete, and of the afternoon sun that would be spilling in onto the blue-and-white tiles, and at once she plowed her way through the dining room into the kitchen. Let's see if John Clark could do as well in the kitchen; there would be no hallowed ground.

John Clark looked around at everything. "What a lovely house," he said. He smiled a sad smile. "How tragic if it should lose its happy charm."

Its happy charm? He obviously knew all about the tragedy of the place; she could hear Rita reveling in all the gory details over steak. "What did you want to talk to me about?" Martha asked him abruptly. Let's see how he counters that!

He sat down in one of the pine chairs at the kitchen table and motioned Martha into the other. She sat.

"Now that I'm here," said John Clark, "I find it oddly difficult to start."

I bet, thought Martha. She stared across the table at him, not helping, not caring, not moving at all. The spider and the fly. The funny thing was, of course, that the one who thought he was the spider had just become the fly.

Pete sat on his side of the front seat of the truck, separated from Connie by the mounds of junk she had pushed beside her as she had moved across. He had stopped talking, and still Connie sat there and waited—waited, he could tell, for him to say something else. Goddammit, why should it be up to him to say something? Shouldn't she say something? Shouldn't she say a whole lot? She had opened the door, and one long, tan leg was now sliding out of it. She wasn't going to say a word! All of a sudden, Pete reached across the long seat of the truck and grabbed her by the elbow and yanked her back.

"Listen," he said. He was half shouting. "Why'd you come back here, anyway? What do you want out of me?"

"Want out of *you!*" And just like that she was shouting back at him. "I came here to give you a message from Sarah. I came here to tell you that Sarah has information."

"I don't mean now, and you know it! I mean, why did you come back *here?* Why did you—"

"What have you got, an ego the size of a house? You think the minute I set foot on this island it has everything to do with *you?*"

Pete was so furious he wanted to hit something. He wanted to hit *her*. She yanked at the door for a second time, and Pete grabbed hold of her again and yanked her back. It wasn't something he had ever done before—yank at Connie—and it occurred to him as she came back into the middle of the seat with the force of his pull and landed on an oil filter that she would come around swinging. Yes, she did: He caught her fist in his free hand and held her an arm's length away.

"What did you think, then, coming back here? Did you think in this place we could avoid each other? Or did you think we'd be friends? Those are the two choices left. Don't answer me. I don't want to hear it. I don't want to hear you saying it—that after everything that's been between us, you expected to be friends!"

Connie opened her mouth.

"Don't!" He let go of her and faced the front. He twisted the key in the ignition. "Get out, please. I have to go find Martha."

Connie got out of the truck. Pete backed around, and as he was hunting for first gear again, she appeared in his window.

"You're a bastard, Pete, you know that?"

Right. Me. Everything is always my fault.

"You think you have it all figured out. Well, you don't!"

Pete looked at her, for a minute fooled into thinking there were actually tears in her eyes; but as he pulled out and looked again, through the side-view mirror, he saw she was standing in the dust in front of Knackie's, chucking him the bird.

Chapter
22

Martha looked at John Clark. He, in turn, was watching her closely.

"Am I making you nervous?" he asked. "You seem to be nervous."

She was about to the point where enough was enough. "I have to be moving along," she said. "If you had something to say . . ."

John Clark looked around the kitchen. "I don't blame you for wishing to leave this house. I can imagine you were unhappy here."

Oh, Jesus, Martha said to herself. Is this guy a flake or what? She stood up. "I do have to go," she said.

John Clark continued to sit in his chair, watching her.

Now what? thought Martha. What an idiot she was to bring him here. It was her own stupid fault if she was now going to be unable to get him out. She moved toward the dining room. "I do have to leave."

Steps behind her. A hand on her arm.

"Please, Martha. Not yet. Sit with me, please."

Martha turned around. There was something in the face . . .

"Please?" He moved back toward the kitchen table.

Pulled by his eyes, Martha followed and sat down.

There they were: The island's two squad cars and the chief's Scout and the fire crew. Pete could see them through the trees, combing the white-pine woods for the bottle of pills. He didn't stop. He continued on past Main Street, past the Whiteaker, and onto the road to the boathouse; but Martha's car was gone and his mind was losing its focus. *What have you got, an ego the size of a house?* He turned around and headed for Factotum. Rita was gone, which was good: He had had enough grizzly encounters for one day. *You're a bastard, Pete.* He seemed to be having an awful lot of bad days lately; was he going to get more used to them after a while? The first thing Pete did once he hit his own kitchen was to go to the refrigerator for a beer, and that bothered him a bit, but there were so many things bothering him that it soon slipped down on the list and out of reach. He worked his way halfway through the beer, sitting at the table, staring at the phone and wondering who he should call. Sarah? *Last I looked, Connie can read.* And besides, Connie might answer. *You think the minute I set foot on this island it has everything to do with you?* Martha; he could try to call Martha. *Could you at least do this for me?* And besides, Martha wasn't home. Pete's head was beginning to ache again, and its aching reminded him of the morning and how this bad day had begun bad right from the beginning. But at least there was something he could do about one part of it. He picked up the phone and called Rita. As soon as she heard his voice she stifled a sob, and Pete put down his beer and sat up.

"Listen, Rita, about this morning, about dinner . . ."

"Oh, for heaven's sake!" Rita cried. "I don't care about this morning. I don't care about this dinner. As if I can't allow you *one lousy day* in all the years I've known you!"

"So what's the matter? Maxine?" Pete found that over the years his sympathy waxed and waned between the rebellious daughter and the stifling mother, while his affection for both parties remained strong, and it was sometimes a great disadvantage.

"Maxine?" Rita sounded confused. "She isn't over there *bothering* you again?"

"No." Pete rubbed his head and reached for his beer. "And she's not a bother. I just thought this morning . . ."

"Oh, *that.*" A loud sniffle at the other end. "It's those World War II movies you've got her watching now. She told me I was acting like one of those women in the bomb factories, chasing after anything in pants."

Pete made a noble effort not to laugh. "So what's wrong?"

"It's John."

So that was it. He *was* married, and he'd finally told her.

"He was supposed to be here at four o'clock.

He was annoyed when you and Martha canceled; I know he was.''

So Martha had canceled also. So he'd been right. At least he knew a brush-off when he saw one.

"At least she came up with an *excuse:* She's leaving. But we were going out anyway, just the two of us, and he said he was coming by at four. At *four,* and it is now six o'clock! I called his room at the Whiteaker a couple of times, but he doesn't answer. I was just wondering if I should go over there, but I think it would look a bit tacky: me chasing after him like that, especially if he were right there in his room.'' A weighted pause followed.

Pete polished off his beer and stood up. "How about if I run over?"

"Oh, *Pete,* would you?"

Pete said he would. He promised to call Rita as soon as he knew something. He contemplated telling her about Bill but decided against it: He would tell Rita when he knew what was going to happen to Bill.

The first thing Pete did at the Whiteaker was to scan the lot in hopes of seeing Bill's Rabbit safe and sound, but it wasn't there. He went into the lobby and asked a familiar-looking high-school student at the desk for John Clark's room number, looking around the lobby for Bill at the same time, and he was only half listening when the desk clerk told him there was no one registered there by that name.

"John Clark," he repeated.

The boy shook his head. "Not here."

Pete sighed. "John Clark. Tall. Distinguished. Late fifties or so. Gray hair, receding at the temples, drives a . . ." A what? Pete tried to picture the rear of the car as it drove off with Rita, repeatedly, at lunch. "Audi. Connecticut plates."

The boy stared at Pete. "Y'mean Harold Stern?"

Martha stared and stared at John Clark.

"That's why I came to Nashtoba, Martha: to look for you." He gave a laugh that was a mixture of many things—nervousness, high excitement. "Of course, I never expected to find you *here*. I expected Edna to divulge some facts that would send me searching for my daughter elsewhere." He leaned forward across the table and placed a long, cool hand over Martha's. She snatched hers back. "I know you blame me for not doing this sooner, for not trying to find you a long time ago."

Martha stood up. This was definite loony-tunes stuff. "I don't know what you're talking about," she said. "My father is dead."

John Clark smiled. He stood up and took a hesitant step toward her, but as Martha shrank back against the kitchen counter he backed right down. "All right, Martha. We can do this all a step at a time. After all, we have all the time in the world now, don't we?"

Martha didn't speak. She pressed herself against the counter harder and harder, its edge pressing into the small of her back. Is this real? Am I awake? she wondered. The counter's edge hurt her. Yes, she was awake.

"I want you to know that I wanted to marry your mother—I wanted to marry her from the first minute she told me you were on the way. And she *wanted* to marry me, Martha. She really did want to. But I wasn't here—and if I'd been here I could have made sure of it; but I wasn't here. It's important that you understand that. That is the very first, the most important thing: that you understand that it was never my wish, never your mother's wish, that we ever be apart, you and I. It was Edna, Martha, who forced her own will upon the rest of us, twisting Lizzie's mind, making Lizzie say things to me, write things to me that she didn't really mean. It took some time for me to sort it out, and by the time I did, by the time I could get back here, it was too late, and you were gone. They wouldn't let me see Lizzie. They told me she didn't want to see me, but I know now that it was never true; never. But back then I believed them. I believed them and I left. I never knew who you were; I never did, not until I came here and talked to Edna that day. You can't blame me for that, can you? *Do* you blame me?''

"No," said Martha. It seemed to be an easy thing to say. She had no idea what he was talking about; not really. He was the father of Lizzie's baby? He was Harold Stern? But he seemed to think this had something to do with Martha. He kept looking at her that way, he kept mixing up the people. But he was the father of Lizzie's baby. "Where is Lizzie's baby?" she asked him.

John Clark's eyes opened wide. "She's here, Martha. She's you! You're my daughter!"

"Tall," said Pete again. "Gray hair, always in a suit. A dark green Audi, Connecticut plates."

The kid was looking scared now, but he repeated

"Harold Stern," flipping and flipping through his register, finally turning the opened book around so Pete could see for himself: Harold Stern; Fairfield, Connecticut. He had registered at the Whiteaker on June 14 at 9:00 P.M. June 14.

June 14. June 14. June 14. The night before Edna died. The night before a dark green car was seen on Shore Road; on that particular night Harold Stern came here and checked into the Whiteaker under his own name. At what point after that did he start to go around calling himself John Clark? And why? After he smacked into the back of Martha's VW? When? When was that? After June 15, obviously; several days after. No, almost a week after, because by then Pete had already talked to Martha, had already gone to see Willy about the water, had met Martha for lunch and had discussed the job about the cousin. But he had arrived June 14. "He just arrived today for the summer," Rita had told Pete. So why lie? And why John Clark? He checked in here before Edna died, telling the truth about his name; after she died, he was lying, and Pete could think of only one clear-cut reason for it—although it didn't make sense on any level.

He turned and strode across the lobby to the phone and called Willy at the station. Was he back from the woods? He was.

"Listen," said Pete.

"Brixton's," said Willy.

"Listen," said Pete again.

"The pills," said Willy, "were Brixton's. I thought you'd want to know."

"Thanks," said Pete. "Now listen. There's a guy running around the island calling himself John Clark. He drives a dark green Audi with Connecti-

231

cut plates. He's tall, gray-haired . . ." Pete was getting pretty darned sick of him, as a matter of fact. "You better find him and check out his tires. And prints."

"What the hell for?"

"His car is dark *green*," said Pete.

"Oh," said Willy. "So that explains it. How thick of me."

Pete took the phone away from his ear and looked at it and put it back.

"The print under the toilet seat. Was it Bill's?"

Silence.

"Was it, damn it? I tell you, this guy came here June 14, he calls himself John Clark, he—"

"The print wasn't your friend Bill's. That still leaves a lot of room for doubt that it belongs to somebody from Connecticut who happened to arrive here on—"

"His name is Hal," said Pete. "Harold Stern."

"Oh," said Willy.

"Will you find him?"

Silence.

"If you don't, I will."

"I'll look into it," said Willy, fast.

Pete glared at the phone again, hung it up, and called Rita.

"He's not here at the hotel," he said, doing his best to keep his voice even. "His car is gone. I've spoken to Will McOwat, and he's going to check around, make sure there wasn't an accident or anything. I'm going to look around a bit myself."

"Thank you," said Rita. "If he's with another woman, will you run him over, please?"

"Gladly," said Pete, with enough behind it for

Rita to holler "Hey!" before he hung up the phone.

Pete got back in the truck and considered which way to turn. *She's leaving,* Rita had said.

She's gone?

Martha hadn't been counting, but it seemed it was the third or the fourth time he had said it.

"She stole you, Martha. It was as good as if she stole you. When I found Edna and I told her what I wanted, she broke right down and told me the whole story, the whole sad truth of what she had done, and I think it was good for her; I think she had been waiting a long time to tell someone, Martha. She told me all about how she and Frank took you away from Lizzie and me. I was going to go right off to Boston to try to find you, but then it dawned on me after what happened that you would, of course, have to eventually come here."

Martha looked out the window at the sea and the darkening sky and tried to put the pieces where they belonged, but her brain didn't seem to be functioning. "The letter on the desk, signed Hal?"

"Hal Stern. This is myself, Martha. You see, don't you, that after what happened I couldn't just walk up to you and let on who I was. Of course, I should have taken that letter away, but I didn't think of it. Edna brought it out to show me; she had saved it and read it over and over again and tortured herself with it for years—she told me so. She kept trying to read it a different way, you see; kept trying to make me out not to love your mother. But it would only tell the truth, and it could only show Edna how wrong she had been. Isn't it odd? Of all of Lizzie's things, that was

233

the only thing she was not able to destroy. But I remembered about the letter later, and I felt it prudent to lie low, so to speak. I followed you, you know. For days. And that day at the restaurant I couldn't wait any longer; I needed to hear your voice, needed to have you look at me and call me Father. I was backing out to follow you when I got that marvelous idea that very minute—what better way to meet you! I backed into you, and that was that."

"That was *what?*" asked Martha crossly. "You said you were John Clark. It didn't exactly—"

"Of course I did. I couldn't tell you who I really was; I couldn't tie myself in to that house, to you, to Edna. Not until I knew what they were going to do. You're very like her, do you know that? You're very like your Lizzie."

Martha turned her back and stared at the rack of knives on the wall. "I don't understand," she said, "what it mattered who you were. You backed into us. You took Rita for a drink. You—"

John Clark chuckled. Harold Stern chuckled. "Don't you see, Martha, it was *you* I wanted to take for a drink? But it worked out best this way. I never planned on Rita being so . . . helpful, shall we say? She told me all about you. It was the neatest thing of all: You had hired her company to find Lizzie's baby; she knew everything I could have possibly wanted to know—everything! Everything except that most important thing: that I was your father, Martha."

"My father is dead," said Martha. A chair scraped behind her. Two hands bore into her upper arms.

"I *told* you," he said, and all of a sudden he

didn't sound so friendly. *"I'm* your father. And I expect you to appreciate everything I've done— everything I've done for *you."*

The tomato box and what looked ike Martha's knapsack were sitting in the middle of the kitchen floor; Pete could see them clearly through the glass. So she had not yet gone; she wasn't off the island yet. So what was the next best thing to do? He was torn between the two choices: trying to talk to Martha one more time before she left and trying to find Harold Stern.

But where would Martha most likely be? The only place that came to mind was The Spookhouse, and somehow he couldn't quite see her wanting to return there; but still, he had so few other choices. *I have to meet someone.* Of course, there was someone else, wasn't there? And what if she were saying good-bye to that someone else before she left? What if they were now together? What if they were leaving together? Suddenly he thought of Connie and Glen Newcomb, and for the second time that day he wanted to hit someone, but he was no longer sure just whom.

Martha twisted out of his fingers. "It's not quite clear to me just what it is that you have done for me," she said. "You came here, you rammed into my car, you—"

"I *freed* you," he said.

Martha gripped the back of her chair and looked down at the table. Freed me?

"Rita told me everything that Edna hadn't, and Edna had already told me enough," said John. "I knew that you hated her—Edna told me so herself,

235

but Rita confirmed it. And I was so proud of you when she said that: You should have hated her—she robbed you of your family, your real family. And Edna also admitted she as good as killed your mother. Maybe she didn't pick up the pills and put them in her mouth, but she drove her to it. Oh yes, she told me how Lizzie wanted you back, was going to fight to get you back. And she would have succeeded, too; she would have called me—I know she would have—and together we would have succeeded. It would have been the three of us again, but Edna ruined it. She ruined everything.'' He was back at the table himself now, leaning over it, leaning over her. "She was drunk, Martha. I told her to stop drinking, she was setting you such an example; but all she would do was laugh and pour another. I asked her right out, Martha, why she hadn't let Lizzie have you back, and do you know what she told me? She told me she couldn't bear the thought of losing you. *She* couldn't! Didn't she once think of us? What about Lizzie and me? You see what that woman was, don't you, Martha? She never thought of anyone but herself, and she as good as killed Lizzie. She drove her to it, killed her, and think what she did to you! Drove someone she called her own daughter to such a hatred that everyone knew of it—everyone on the whole island, or so Rita says. And do you know what else? I told her I was surprised to see her here in this same house after so many years, and do you know what she told me? She told me she had to stay here, because she knew the minute she left the house that she would never see you again. You see? It's just as well she's dead. It's no wonder you hate it here; but we'll be leaving here soon ourselves, don't worry."

"Leaving?" asked Martha.

"Home, Martha. Home to Connecticut. We've lost thirty-four years, but none of that matters right now. From now on you and I are—"

Martha pushed away from the table and headed toward the door. "I have to go, really," she said.

"Oh, not yet, Martha," said Hal. He reached out and pulled her around by the arm so that they were facing each other again. "We'll go, but not just yet. Please."

He was halfway up Shore Road when he remembered about Rita and that her house was the next logical place for this Harold Stern to show, and the thought of him walking into her house and pretending once again that he was this John Clark character set Pete's teeth on edge. Maybe he should be heading to Rita's to head him off there. Or should he call Willy and have him get himself over to Rita's and pick him up? If he were even considering picking him up, a move Pete was still not completely convinced he'd make. *You think you have it all figured out.* Pete almost laughed. As if there was anyone who knew more clearly what he *didn't* have figured out!

He swung the truck off into the soft shoulder, spun his wheels getting out, turned around, and headed for Rita's. *You're a bastard, Pete, you know that?* No, he didn't. But that was only one other thing in a long line of things he didn't know.

How clearly she could see it now, now when she was passing the point of reason. Her mother—

or, rather, Edna, who was not really her mother—
taking her away, fighting to keep her, spending
how many years unable to face up to either the
decision or the daughter, consequently pushing her
daughter further out of her sight. No wonder her
father, after years of walking that delicate fence
between them, found it necessary to be gone so
much. Oh, the ghosts in this house! The dead Lizzie first. Martha put a hand to her hair. Do I look
like her? she wondered. And she knew as she wondered that she did: knew it by remembering the
look on her mother's face when she walked into
the room in a different sweater, with her hair
pinned up. Oh, what that look had done! It sent
Martha spinning off into agony over what she had
said this time to make her mother look that way,
and her father always fading away, leaving her to
face that other look alone.

Martha snapped herself back to the present and
to the stranger across the table who was planning
out her future life.

"It's a lovely house, but I know very well how
hard it would be for you to remain here, and it's
best just to get rid of it, don't you think? And since
we still don't know what the police are going to
do, it might be better for you and I to be gone
from here fairly soon. I certainly don't think it will
ever dawn on them that I was here then, of course,
but just to be on the safe side . . ."

Martha struggled over his words for a minute
and then sat up straighter. "You came here?"

"I told you, Martha. I came here to talk to
Edna. To find you. She was drinking, she was
really not her old self, not Edna as I remembered
her. She told me it all—everything: how she took

you, how she drove Lizzie to her death, how she let us all believe she drowned. She had become a horrible person, Martha. You're glad, aren't you? Glad I did what I did? Why are you looking like that? I knew right away you'd be glad, of course; but then after Rita told me how you really felt, I knew I could talk to you and it would be all right. Of course, I tried to stop her drinking at first, but she kept right on talking and talking and drinking. Then I went upstairs to use the bathroom and there were those pills there, and how neat could it possibly be? I could do to her what she had made Lizzie do. Nothing was easier; nothing in my life ever seemed so . . . meant to be. I took her glass from her and went into the dining room to pour another, and at the same time I emptied out the capsules in the glass and stirred them in. I was afraid it would taste awful, or that it would take too long, but nothing like that happened at all. She drank it—of course she drank it! And she tumbled off the couch not twenty minutes later. I waited, to be sure, and then I retraced my steps to make sure I left no signs of my presence, but I really never thought about the letter until afterward, and then I felt it best not to walk around calling myself Hal. You can see that, I'm sure." He stopped then and frowned. "I confess to you I did not understand and do not understand this business about the bathtub." All of a sudden his face lit up as he looked at her. "Or was it you, Martha? Were you trying to help? Did you think she might still be alive? Were you the one who put her in the tub?"

"No," said Martha. She was feeling sick.

"Well, don't look so worried, Martha. I'll be all right, you'll be all right, we'll leave for Connecticut soon, and no one will ever be the wiser. I'm your father. I'll—''

Martha pushed back her chair and stood up. Her legs, her hands, even her eyes, seemed to be shaking; she couldn't quite focus on his face. "My father is dead," said Martha, "and you killed my mother, and you actually think I would go anywhere with you after that?"

He was mad. Completely mad. She looked into his face and watched his eyes turn gray and cold, and she knew then that she had just made a very big mistake.

Rita's house was all the way back by the causeway, and by the time Pete got there he had already convinced himself that that was now the last place that John Clark would show. John Clark was probably long gone by now. Yes, there was no green Audi in Rita's drive. Pete shot out of the truck and raced up the drive, trying to think of just the right thing to say to Rita to keep her calm, while at the same time making sure she would stay far away from Clark; and lying, it seemed, was the thing that was going to work best. Luckily for Pete, who had never mastered the art, Rita did most of the work for him.

She took one look at Pete's face and began. "I knew it. Okay, who was it? Who was he with? Was it Martha?"

Martha! And what prompted Rita to pick her particular name out of the hat? But he had only to halfheartedly deny it to find that, perversely, it did the trick.

"I knew it! I mean, I really did know it in a certain unknown way. He was too interested! He asked too many questions about her, and this business of dinner seemed all out of proportion to . . . That does it. I mean this really does it." She turned and slammed one of her immaculately polished cupboard doors and snatched up a straw bag from the kitchen counter and shoved past Pete toward the door.

"Where are you going?" He had rarely seen her this upset.

"I'm certainly not going to be sitting here waiting, when and if he decides to show," she said. "I'll go out drinking. I'll go to California. I'll go shopping!"

And that was all Pete needed to hear. Pete followed her Dodge Omni as far as the causeway turn, and when she turned right to go over it, he turned left onto Shore Road and once again set out for The Spookhouse to find Martha.

There was the house ahead of him, a black mass of angles against a lighter gray sky; and involuntarily, it seemed, he slowed the truck and crept closer. Yes, this was the house, and there was Martha's little yellow car, and . . . He couldn't quite believe it. Beside her Volkswagen was the Audi with the Connecticut plates. Someone else. John Clark. Harold Stern. And whatever he had wanted to talk to Martha about didn't seem to make much sense any more. He jammed his sneaker down on the gas with a week-long, month-long, year-long pent-up fury and blew past The Spookhouse in a spray of sand.

Martha tried to backtrack. She stood up from the table, tried to smile, tried to maneuver herself nearer to the door. She had fooled around talking

to this crazy man long enough, and it was time to
get out. "Of course you're right," she said to him.
"There is nothing to hold me here, after all. And
Connecticut might be . . ."

He rose with her, moved with her, kept his body
between Martha and the door. He watched her
speaking, watched her voice fade away, and slowly
shook his head.

"Oh, Martha," he said. "No. I see what you're
thinking about me. I can see just what you're thinking of doing, and it isn't going to Connecticut,
now, is it?" He laughed. "So I'm a fool! Again,
I'm a fool! I don't know why I expected anything
different. You're not coming to Connecticut. Are
you?"

Martha tried to get away from him, backing up
farther, and she backed herself up against the
table. "I'd like to talk about it more," she said,
and Harold Stern laughed again.

"Talk about it. Yes. All right, Martha, let's sit
down and talk about it. You sit there, and I'll sit
here, and I'll watch you, and you'll watch me, and
the minute I look away you'll run to the phone and
call your friend the policeman, won't you?"

Martha shook her head. O God.

"Won't you?" He pulled back her chair and
pushed her into it. "The answer, Martha? No, you
won't. Okay. Now, let's talk about it, you and I."

Harold Stern began to talk. How long did they
sit there, how many hours had this been? He was
off on some other track now, some other life of
his, something that had spurred this leap out of
that other life and back into her own.

"When she left me she cost me the boys," he
was saying now. "I don't know how it happened,

I don't know how she made that judge believe her lies! He denied me my rights, he denied me my children! As if I would ever hurt *them!* . . . She said she was going to make sure I never touched her again, as if it was my fault those things that happened. I never meant to hurt her. I would never have laid a finger on her if she had only been more . . . *loving* towards me. She took the boys from me, she took herself from me, she said terrible things about me, she took everything. But I didn't love her, Martha—not really, not ever, not the way I loved your mother or the way I loved you. It was best that she left me, really; it was the chance I'd been waiting for all my life: to come find you and put my rightful family back together once again—my real family, my first one. Don't you see?"

"I see," said Martha. "Yes, I do see, and I think we could explain this. I could go with you, and—"

Harold Stern smashed a long, delicate hand down onto the table, pushed himself up from the chair, and lurched toward her. Martha jumped up and ran for the door. He caught her and threw her behind him back into the kitchen, sending her crashing into the wall by the bay window, and she screamed and fell to the floor.

Chapter
23

Pete was unsure just how far away from The Spookhouse his anger had taken him when it began to pull him back. Who did she think she was, anyway? Whose big idea *was* all this? It was bad enough that Pete had been drawn into this mess himself, but why pick on Rita? Why go after the one person on the whole island who was actually making somebody happy? And what about Bill Freed? She deserved to know about Bill Freed. She deserved to know how she had ruined his life, how she was about to ruin Rita's. Wait a minute! Had Pete forgotten for a minute the shady nature of the man who was supposedly making Rita so happy? Rita, who had been in tears for most of the entire day. Martha deserved to know about that also, deserved to know that this man she was holed up with in her mother's house had possibly . . . probably . . .

He plowed into the drive of the Spookhouse and slammed to a stop an inch or two away from the Audi. He bolted out of the truck and up the steps, feeling ready to kill her. He pounded against the wooden door and it burst open, crashing into the wall behind it, and then he heard her scream.

They were in the kitchen. *His* kitchen. *Their* kitchen. He took one look at her, crumpled up under the window into a spindly-looking ball, saw a long arm in an expensive suit reaching back-handed for another blow, and he sprang off the balls of his feet into the air and onto the arm, taking the man down with it.

He never saw the knife. He never noticed that the knife rack was missing its heaviest blade; he felt only the exploding anger, and then an excruciating pain in his side, and then a certain silliness. He was down on the floor, the same floor upon which he had once been so happily wrestling with Martha, but this time he was wrestling with Harold Stern, a man who must have been close to sixty years old and entrapped in a business suit and loafers besides, and Pete was losing! He couldn't understand it. He couldn't seem to move his right arm at all, and any kind of twisting motion filled his chest with this terrible pain. He couldn't push the man up and off him. He couldn't seem to catch a good breath. Then Martha was looming over them with a wine bottle in her hand, and all he could think of was, I hope it's not the Bordeaux. And then it didn't matter what it was. She cracked it into the edge of the kitchen counter, and as Pete lay helpless on the floor, she began to hack up Hal Stern with the bottle's broken edge.

It seemed like a long trip to Oz—which would have been all right, if he didn't keep running into the darned field of poppies. He couldn't keep his eyes open. Every time he opened them he saw a witch, but he was having trouble figuring out just which witch it was. She was beautiful, so it seemed that she must be the good witch; but she was making him feel uncomfortable in some way, making him want to look around for those flying monkeys. She told him he was not a bastard. She told him that a few times. Finally, on one of his sorties out of the poppies, he saw the pale gold hair, and he said, "Martha?"

"Not exactly. As a matter of fact, nobody seems to know just where Martha is. Not that anybody's doing much looking . . ."

Connie. Pete tried to sit up and found it was a serious mistake. Pain through the poppies.

"Hey!" Connie hollered. "Stay down there or they'll kick me out. They only let me in because I said I was your wife."

Pete looked around him. Hospital walls. Bradford Hospital? "What happened?" he asked.

"At the risk of sounding overly dramatic," said Connie, "Martha sliced through that guy Stern's carotid artery in a valiant effort to save your life. He bought the farm, but most of the island seems to think you were worth it: They've been hanging around here for hours on end."

"Who?"

Connie gave a snort. "Who *not*, would be the better question. Sarah's stomping up and down the hall yelling at the nurses, and Rita's crying all over everyone, and Hardy Rogers keeps blowing in and out to make sure they don't kill you, and Bill Freed keeps trying to take Sarah home, and those two crazy twins are—"

Pete closed his eyes. "Martha is . . . gone?"

There was a silence of some length.

"Bert Barker says he passed the VW as he was coming back on-island from over on the Hook. They think she took off in all the commotion over the two bodies. Must have thought they were going to arrest her for killing her father; but if you ask my opinion and anyone else's opinion, it was self-defense. Or *your* defense, anyway."

Pete opened his eyes and looked at the wall. "*Two* bodies?"

Again a silence of some length. Then Connie coughed a couple of times and spoke up. "No offense, Pete, but you didn't look too good by the time the rescue got there. They *thought* it was two bodies." She gave a violent cough and shifted in her chair. "But I was pleased to announce to your adoring public not more than two hours ago that the Official Word is that you're going to live."

Pete closed his eyes and opened them again at once. "Her *father?*"

"Her father. Hal Stern. Old Edna and Frank adopted Lizzie's baby. Martha. That's what Sarah wanted to tell you."

Her father. Self-defense. Pete closed his eyes again and saw, again, Martha turning a bottle into a blade and swinging it at Stern, not once, not even twice, but again and again and again. There had been blood everywhere, all over everything. Pete had reached out his one movable arm to stop her; he had wanted to stop her, but he had been unable to hold his arm up, let alone do much of anything with it, and still she kept chopping at the man.

"Hey!" Connie hollered at him from about an inch above his nose, and Pete opened his eyes with a painful jerk and Connie jumped back. "Jesus

Christ! If you're going to go shutting your eyes you should take a deep breath now and then!" She walked away and said "Jesus" once again, but much more quietly, from someplace else.

"It hurts when I breathe."

Connie came back to him and looked down, frowning. "Maybe I should call the doctor."

"No," said Pete.

"Maybe you'd prefer that I go?"

"No," said Pete, again.

"That's what they *say* happened," said Bert. "Course, I still say Martha killed Edna as well as that fella Stern."

Ed Healey looked sideways at Bert. "Ya s'pose . . ."

"They found Stern's fingerprints on Edna's toilet seat," said Evan quietly, from his corner on the bench. "And his tracks in her drive. And the pills they found in the woods were Brixton's, not Hardy's."

"Then why'd she run, huh, Ev? Stern was self-defense. That's all Pete kept blabberin', the whole time he was in and out on the way to the hospital. The Bean wasn't goin' to lock her up for that."

"S'pose not," said Ed Healey, and this time he looked at Evan. But Evan was staring into his Coke bottle, and he didn't even look up.

"Poor ole Rita," said Bert. He chuckled. "Guess she made some fool of herself, all right."

"She's doin' all right," said Evan. "Least she will, if ya leave her alone."

"Oh ho! And how do *you* know, Ev? Ya been rewirin' her phone?"

Evan didn't answer. He stood up and moved off the porch, down the steps, and toward his truck.

"Hey, Bert," said Ed Healey. "Ya ever get that fence fixed?"

"Nah," said Bert. "I tell ya. And The Bean's so mad at Bill he's never goin' to let him out, and who knows when Pete'll be back up to his game? . . . *Lord,* I wish he'd hire somebody so's we'd get a few things done 'round this place!"